A Modern Parable

MICHAEL SEATON with **JOHN BLASE**

■ **ZONDERVAN**®

ZONDERVAN.com/
AUTHORTRACKER
follow your favorite authors

ZONDERVAN

Start with Me
Copyright © 2010 by Michael R. Seaton

This title is also available as a Zondervan ebook. Visit www.zondervan.com/ebooks.

This title is also available in a Zondervan audio edition. Visit www.zondervan.fm.

Requests for information should be addressed to:
Zondervan, *Grand Rapids, Michigan 49530*

Library of Congress Cataloging-in-Publication Data

Seaton, Mike.
   Start with me : a modern parable / Mike Seaton, with John Blase.
         p.   cm. — (Start)
   Includes bibliographical references.
   ISBN 978-0-310-32584-0 (pbk.)
   I. Blase, John. II. Title.
PS3619.E2575S73 2010
813'.6—dc22   2009051039

The overall setting for this story is the very real city of Santa Fe, New Mexico, including the campus of The College of St. John's and its immediate surroundings. However, all characters and events are purely fictional.

Published in association with the literary agency of Alive Communications, Inc., 7680 Goddard Street, Suite 200, Colorado Springs, CO 80920. www.alivecommunications.com

Cover design: Curt Diepenhorst
Cover photography: Jeff Casemier
Interior design: Ben Fetterley

Printed in the United States of America

10 11 12 13 14 15 /DCI/ 21 20 19 18 17 16 15 14 13 12 11 10 9 8 7 6 5 4 3 2 1

Contents

Also by Michael Seaton

start> Becoming a Good Samaritan DVD curriculum,
hosted by John Ortberg

start> Becoming a Good Samaritan Participant's Guide,
with Ashley Wiersma

Start with Me

Dedication/ Acknowledgments

Start with Me is dedicated to Mercy. God's mercy offered freely to all of us and by extension the mercy we ought offer to everyone we encounter. For …

> *The quality of mercy is not strain'd,*
> *It droppeth as the gentle rain from heaven*
> *Upon the place beneath. It is twice blest:*
> *It blesseth him that gives and him that takes.*
>
> —*Shakespeare, The Merchant of Venice*

I would also like to acknowledge some folks …

First of all my wife, Carla, who said, "If this is what God wants you to do, then you better do it."

Kate and Alex, my children. Because they'll think it is so cool to have their names in the front of a book—and what dad could ignore that!

John Blase, my coauthor, for his willingness to take chances, to work with me on a story that would touch the heart and not a "how to" book.

Greg Clouse, my editor at Zondervan, who is one of the most patient and helpful guys I know.

Mike Salisbury, my Zondervan marketing guy and Dream-weaver.

T.J. Rathbun and John Raymond, my longtime Zondervan buddies. You guys believed in this right from the beginning and I needed that as the months rolled by.

Jared Yaple, my erstwhile start> companion. He's working hard everyday to put flesh on my bones.

Lee Hough from Alive Communications. It's always a comfort to hear his Texas drawl lay hands of assurance with a simple, "Hey bud, how ya doin'?"

Finally, to my C2 compadres. For handling the day-to-day back at the ranch so I could ride the range and dream. Thanks Andy, Chad, Katie, Stacia, Kaylee, Jim, Steve, Dora, Michael, David, Mark, David, and all you Web Team folks.

It was the best of times, it was the worst of times, it was the age of wisdom, it was the age of foolishness, it was the epoch of belief, it was the epoch of incredulity, it was the season of Light, it was the season of Darkness, it was the spring of hope, it was the winter of despair, we had everything before us, we had nothing before us, we were all going direct to Heaven, we were all going direct the other way ...

— Charles Dickens, *A Tale of Two Cities*

Author's Preface

Consistently living out the teachings of Jesus has never been easy for any of us! But the teaching that has always troubled me the most, and the one that I believe is a huge challenge for the church, is Jesus' command in the parable of the Good Samaritan to "love our neighbor."

If we are to be the hands and feet of Jesus in the world today — the visible image of the invisible God — if we are to love our neighbor, seek justice and mercy, and walk humbly with God, then it seems to me, to borrow Charles Dickens' words, we need to leave our "best of times" neighborhoods and find out what life is really like in the "worst of times" neighborhoods.

It was that conviction and God's prompting in late August 2006 that started me down the road to developing a teaching tool that might help people like myself actually live out our faith not just on Sunday, but Monday through Saturday too!

And for the next three years of my life, God used my twenty-plus years of video production and corporate training skills, along with my experiences working on DVD curriculums with some of the best Christian writers, thinkers, and teachers, to create start> Becoming a Good Samaritan. It features more than sixty inspiring interviews with leaders including Archbishop Desmond Tutu, Eugene Peterson, Philip Yancey, Kay Warren,

Lynne Hybels, John Perkins, Princess Zulu, Rob Bell, Shane Claiborne, Brenda Salter McNeil, Charles Colson, Jim Cymbala, Hor-
ace Smith, and Joni Earekson Tada — all talking about what it
means to be a Good Samaritan.

So how does that curriculum fit with the book you're holding
in your hands? When my coauthor John Blase and I discussed a
companion book for the curriculum, at first we thought, "Let's
just take some of the best interviews and real Good Samaritan
stories from my research and make that the book." But then we
realized that as much as people are inspired by the likes of the
Christian leaders on the DVD and the stories of others, we often
have a hard time putting ourselves in their shoes. We think, "Of
course it's easy for *them*, but we're just average Christians. What
difference can we possibly make?"

The more we thought about it, the more we kept coming
back to the idea that the companion book needed to be about
the struggles that you and I face. Trying to be all that God wants
us to be in the midst of family, jobs, kids, and busy, busy, busy. It
couldn't be about the wonderful success stories of people who
have figured out what it means to be a Good Samaritan — it
had to be about the rest of us, trying to begin, trying to start.

That's when we knew that *Start with Me* had to be a story. A
story with flesh-and-blood characters created from the pages
of our lives, facing the same fears, doubts, concerns, and trou-
bles that you and I face every day.

When you read this book, my hope is that you will find yourself somewhere in these pages. That you will wrestle with the

same questions and concerns as Sam, Phillip, Luci, Elly, Jordan, Jim, and Linda. And that in the end, like them, you will find the desire, the courage, and the conviction to take your faith out of your church and into a desperate world filled with hungry, sick, oppressed, damaged, and lost souls. Neighbors waiting and hoping that someone like you will stop, reach out, touch, and show them ... Love.

— Michael Seaton
May 2010

Prologue

Wednesday's child is full of woe ...

Forgive and forget. Two borders she could not cross. The memory haunted her even now. If she could stay busy it seemed to stay quiet, but she could not always be busy. The remembrance was both sight and sound, always the same: A sky so black it threatened to swallow you. The only lights were the crazed eyes of a woman, her mother, old beyond her years, slowly tearing pages from the Bible, eating them, repeating "taste and see ... the Lord is good ... taste and see."

She was seven when they crossed under the cover of a new moon, led by "coyotes," the code name for the men who guided illegal immigrants into the U.S. There were others in their group but they were told to snake two by two through rocks and sage across the border. They could see the shadows of the others; still her mother was direct: "Don't let go of my hand, Isabel." But something or someone, she never knew what, had spooked the coyote; the group scattered in fear. Mother and daughter ran further into the black. By sunrise everything around them looked the same; it stayed that way for three days. Darkness seemed their only companion.

A small hip-pack had water and crackers, enough for one day, not enough for three. Her mother prayed for miracles more than once. God must have been asleep or busy or just not interested.

On the night of the third day, her mother simply sat down and stopped. Hope was not deferred, but lost. Isabel watched as her mother took out a Bible and began to eat the pages. The last thing she saw her mother do was struggle to swallow the words of God and then the darkness swallowed them both.

The crushing blackness stole her sense of time. The whites of his eyes seemed to appear from nowhere. His arms lifted her and held her close as he ran through the night. She cried for her mother once, but his voiced shushed her: "No. She's dead." She never knew his name; he must have been all of fifteen, but strong. The air smelled like rain, but the drops never fell.

By sunrise Isabel's slender legs burned as she sat on the rusty floor of a van. She could see the road through the holes as they drove; the motion made her sick. A woman packed beside her looked to be her mother's age. She leaned down to Isabel: "The Lord is good, no?" That question had already been answered for a seven-year-old, and nothing Isabel had seen since then caused her to change her mind.

The memory lunged at her tonight as she spied the Gideon Bible on the nightstand. She wondered if the Gideons had ever tried to eat their words. Isabel shook away the thought, gathered her clothes, and quickly dressed.

Like the others, the man in the bed had no name. But this one surprised her by asking *her* name as she reached the door. "Isabel," she said. He sat on the edge of the bed and spoke softly: "Do you know what your name means?" She knew; her mother had made certain Isabel knew. "Yes. It means 'consecrated to God.'"

It had become a rhythm, this offering of herself — a routine she had followed for some time now, years to be accurate. Everything was prearranged, businesslike. From the beginning, she was instructed never to leave anything in the room, personal belongings such as an earring or tube of lipstick. Isabel was always careful that nothing of hers remained, or so she believed.

She sent a text message from outside and the car promptly arrived to retrieve her. Not a word was spoken until the car parked at the edge of campus. The driver handed her an envelope along with a phrase she had long since come to detest: "The Lord is good, no?" Isabel took the envelope and left the car, quickly disappearing into the shadows under the cover of a new moon.

●●●

Pretty — that's the word people used to describe Isabel, they always had. She wished that once, just once, someone would call her *beautiful*, but so far, no one had. She remembered visiting a house, many years ago, and sitting on a porch beside an old woman. The wind was hot, calico kittens were asleep in the front yard, radio music wafted through the open door, the woman had on two different shoes. The reason for being there was unclear; the woman's words, however, were not. She leaned over and whispered to Isabel: "You must suffer to be beautiful." As the years went by, Isabel wondered *how much* she must suffer. But the old woman didn't tell her that. Isabel guessed there must be more.

●●●

For most people, it was just a nice little koi pond in the center of a college campus, but Isabel was not most people. Several years ago, while exploring the campus, she had stumbled upon the pond and stopped to watch a man in a gray uniform knee-deep in the dark water, his hands filled with tools. Isabel asked him what he was doing. Before the man could reply, the koi surfaced and rolled around his legs. They were bright orange and white, thick as the man's arm. Isabel thought they were the most beautiful things she had ever seen. The man spoke to her kindly; he called the fish the "angels of St. John's." Such was his kindness that Isabel found no reason to doubt his word. When she was troubled, which was often, she would visit the koi; she always left lighter, less heavy than when she had arrived. As time passed, she believed them *her angels*.

So on this Wednesday, after having sold herself to yet another man, Isabel sat with legs crossed at the pond's edge. From a distance, you would have thought her a child, but she was no longer a child. She believed *her angels* could understand her thoughts without a word being spoken. The koi would huddle at the pond's edge, just beneath her feet, as if they were listening. Isabel told them her secrets, some of them so filled with pain that the koi would disappear into the shadows, as if the suffering were too much. But they would always reappear. As Isabel would finally stand to leave, the koi knew her parting whisper was always her one great dream: *Just once … called beautiful.*

Thursday

"To lend each other a hand when we're falling," Brendan said. "Perhaps that's the only work that matters in the end."

Frederick Buechner,
Brendan

Samantha Dobbins turned up the volume a little; she thought some Springsteen might help her pass the time — *I had a friend was a big baseball player... back in high school* — but it didn't seem to help. Five o'clock in Santa Fe was always busy, regardless of the season. Traffic congestion fell on the just and unjust. Samantha wasn't sure which one of the two described her today, she didn't really care. All she knew was, "I'm running late." *Glory days, they'll pass you by, glory days ...*

Her finger instinctively hit the search button on the radio. One station north of the Boss was an all-news channel:

"Calls to one DC-area hunger hotline have jumped 248 percent in the last twelve months, most of them from people who have never needed food aid before ... closer to home, Mercy Shelter will close its doors at the end of the month due to a lack of funding, this as the city reports record foreclosures and unemployment. This winter's forecast is more snow than usual, something that does not bode well for many in the area ..."

"Lord, what a mess ... long way from 'glory days.'" She reached again to find another station when she realized she was about to rear-end the pickup stopped in front of her. Samantha slammed on her brakes, drawing the stares of two silver-haired ladies beside her in a Jetta.

Samantha had recently set up a Facebook page; today she was a perfect candidate for that quiz which asks "What color are you?" She wouldn't need to answer the questions because she already knew — RED! The truth was she could have given that answer most days for the last few months, and today was no exception. A lot of things were frustrating her these days, but she knew it wasn't the things themselves but something deeper, something that had been tugging at her for some time now.

The light changed from red to green and back to red again, but the pickup didn't move an inch — neither did Sam. The red light had cycled past them, twice. Now her blood pressure had risen to match the traffic light up ahead. She really didn't have time for this. If the light passed them by once more, she was going to use the horn.

The brightly colored bumper sticker across the truck's back window could not be missed — *I Brake for No Apparent Reason.* "Well, that's nice." She fought the sarcasm and started to lower her window; maybe she could wave and get the driver's attention. As she inched her head out the window, the lyrics coming from the truck slapped her in the face at full volume:

> I've got supper in the oven, a good woman's lovin'
> and one more day to be my little kid's dad.
> Lord knows I'm a lucky man.

And that was all it took, a slight reorientation. She sat back in her seat and her *red* changed to *yellow* — the color of caution. She knew full well that if the gender were switched in that song, the song was hers. She was a lucky woman, married to a good man for fifteen years, mother of four great kids. Supper wasn't in the oven but they were to meet friends tonight at a little place off the plaza, so dinner was taken care of. Samantha Dobbins was a lucky woman. *But if I'm so lucky, why do I feel this way?* she wondered.

The pickup must have pulled forward in her few seconds of self-talk. The light turned green and lucky Samantha watched the traffic signal allow one vehicle, the beater pickup moving at molasses speed, to pass. And then the light and Samantha turned red again.

* * *

Everyone except her mother called her Sam. She was the firstborn of conservative, Baptist, Kansas schoolteachers. Hard-won scholarships gained her entrance to St. John's in Santa Fe; Midwestern persistence gained her the major in Spanish. She spent two years after graduation in Mexico City, where she met Phillip, a disillusioned divinity student. She was teaching, he was searching. It wasn't that Phillip had stopped believing in God; he just wasn't sure God was *awake*. In January of the second year her mentor from St. John's called and asked if she would be interested in returning to teach a few classes. A month earlier, Phillip had asked if she would be interested in being his wife. She happily responded *yes* to both. Sam arranged to live in the women's dormitory for the fall term and began teaching. Phillip followed in October and found a two-bedroom casita for rent. The small house had a tiny balcony upstairs with a striking view of the Sandia Mountains and the red-rock bell tower that they soon learned belonged to the historic Grace Church. Grace did not have the ornate stained glass like so many of the beautiful cathedrals in town, but it had the bell tower. Each evening the chimes would sound at dusk; Sam and Phillip believed something was always realigned when the bells would play. They arranged for their wedding service to be held under the shelter of those mountains and the bells of Grace Church on December 14, 1994. Family and friends attended. Luminaries lined the sidewalk surrounding the church as a light snow fell.

In a blink of time, it seemed, fifteen years had passed, and she had become a fixture at the college, gaining tenure and the first flecks of gray. Phillip had written several volumes of poetry that did moderately well, with guest lectures and workshops in their wake. He was also a contributing writer for a popular outdoors magazine. Their firstborn, Maggie, was now thirteen; Kate was eleven and the twins — Sarah and Lily — were eight. Sam and Phillip had been intentional about the girls choosing one extracurricular activity and no more. They had witnessed the obscene schedule some of their friends kept and wanted nothing to do with it. Still, with one activity multiplied by four directions, they often found themselves feeling driven, gasping for air.

Writing had afforded Phillip the freedom to be very present with the girls in their early years. It had also afforded Sam the ability to continue her teaching load as well as work on her doctorate. She was now Dr. Samantha Dobbins, chair of the department. Sam often wished her parents were around to see their dreams for her come true. Phillip's parents had both died when he was young; an uncle raised him until he left for college. But with Sam it had been different. Her parents had been integral to her world for so long, but then it was as if the center collapsed, leaving only fringe. Her mother died suddenly just two months before Sam received the doctorate degree. Her father grieved almost a year before a stroke damaged his mind. He now lived with Sam's only brother, Ben, back in Kansas and constantly asked, "When's your mother coming home?"

Sam and Phillip had made Grace Church their spiritual home. Before officiating for their wedding ceremony, the rector insisted on several weeks of counseling. Father Duncan so impressed the young couple that they continued attending in the weeks following *I do*. The eclectic congregation gradually became family. The church rejoiced with them at the births and confirmations of their daughters, and also wept with them when Sam lost her mother. Father Duncan had moved on a few years ago, succeeded by Pastor Jordan, a younger, more relaxed minister in title and approach. Sam and Phillip liked his conversational style and insistence on open communion.

Phillip was aging as many men do, gracefully. His gray hair and beard were close cropped, giving him a boyish charm, but his weathered face spoke of experience. Sam spent almost every lunch hour since her last birthday in the college pool, swimming the laps she hoped would keep time at bay. Her body had carried, delivered, and nourished four daughters and now, in her early forties, she was feeling her age. It didn't help that boys were beginning to take notice of Maggie and vice versa. Phillip had recently mentioned "worry lines" at the corners of her eyes; she now saw them every time she looked in the mirror.

It was in this season, in the middle of it all, that Sam began to feel the frustration, something like a low-grade fever. A question kept surfacing in her head: *Isn't there more?* She had heard those words from many people about her age. Chances were good it was the second-half-of-life question: you get to a certain point in life, take a look around, and wonder, *Is this it?* Sam was grateful for the blessings that surrounded her, but she had to admit the question was tempting. *Was there more to the life she was living?*

●●●

Sam's light finally turned green. She had to stop for gas, get home, change into something comfortable, and make sure Elly and the girls were squared away. Elly Jackson was a junior at St. John's who had been over at the house one afternoon last year when Phillip called with surprise tickets to a show. "Oh, Dr. Dobbins, ya'll should go. I'd be happy to watch the girls for a few hours." Ever since that afternoon, Sam and Phillip had been able to enjoy a little more time to themselves or with friends. The girls were completely taken with Elly and her homemade macaroni and cheese and Southern drawl. Alabama born and bred, Elly was a perfect picture of charm and grace. But the wonderful thing about Elly was that she wasn't aware of her grace; she was just being Elly. And Sam, well, she was completely at ease leaving her daughters with someone who regularly used the word *shucks*.

As Sam pulled up to the gas pump, she couldn't believe her eyes. There, not six feet from the front of her Trooper, sat the beater pickup from what seemed like just moments ago. "You have got to be kidding me." No blaring country music this time; however the engine was running. Sam kept her eyes open but never saw anyone get in or out of the truck. The clerk's voice through the tiny speaker on the pump startled her. "Lady, would you please turn off your engine before pumping the gas?"

Sam was embarrassed at her level of distraction. "Sure, sorry about that."

●●●

"Elly, you've got our cell numbers. We should be back by nine."

"Oh, we'll be fiiiinnne, won't we, girls?" Smiles on her daughters' faces answered Elly's question as they followed the Southern pied piper out into the backyard. *Fine* — now that was a word to describe these days. The girls were fine, her marriage was fine, work was fine, church was fine, life was fine. Then her ringtone interrupted her reverie with a text from Phillip: *Running late, meet you there. Love, P.* "Well, fine."

Jim and Linda Fairchild lived across the street back when Sam started the teaching track at St. John's. They were both young married couples just getting started, trying to make ends meet. Misery really doesn't love company, but it does enjoy a select few, so most Thursday evenings found the two couples on the Dobbins' small balcony. They would eat and laugh and dream and bask in the uncommon sun of true friendship. Jim's forte was banking, but it was Linda who was really good with numbers. She scrimped and saved and clipped and co-oped so that a stay-at-home wife never looked frumpy, their cars were paid for, and their twentieth wedding anniversary was spent in Italy. Sam loved the fact that even after their kids had come along and life conspired to pull them apart, they kept to one Thursday each month with these longtime friends. Jim and Linda started attending Grace Church about five years ago, so the Dobbins did see their good friends most Sundays, but it was the Thursday dinners that kept them glued together.

●●●

With Jim and Linda, you could pick up right where you left off. And so they did. Linda went first. "We haven't been able to stop talking about our dinner conversation last month." Jim merged in: "It felt like we just got started and then the evening was over." Though they could laugh with the best of them, when they wanted to talk "serious," it was obvious.

Last month's dinner began with a "surprise" from Jim and Linda; they were giving a lot of thought to trying to adopt a child. Linda had experienced four miscarriages over the early years of their marriage. The last experience stretched the vow of "for better or worse" almost to the breaking point. Her dreams of being a stay-at-home mom turned into nightmares. Her physical recovery was never a problem; her heart, however, always lagged far behind. Sam and Phillip had walked with them through those valleys, awkwardly but faithfully. Sam was carrying a child either before or during each of Linda's miscarriages, so she was a vivid reminder of what Linda could not have. Their faith in God grew differently in those days; the Dobbins' by addition, the Fairchilds' by subtraction. But faith grows nonetheless. Against the odds and due to God's grace, the Fairchilds' marriage and Linda's friendship with Sam stayed intact. But losing those children left Jim and Linda fragile, somewhat resigned, so thoughts of even trying to adopt caught their longtime friends off guard.

The conversation a month ago revolved around Linda's twenty-fifth high school reunion. It had been good to see old classmates, many of them for the first time since graduation. The class valedictorian was a girl named Becky Fisher; smart and involved back then, and seemingly little had changed. She was invited to speak for the evening and used the opportunity to introduce three little girls, all orphaned by the HIV/AIDS epidemic in sub-Saharan Africa, but more amazingly all of them adopted by Becky and her family. She didn't have a PowerPoint presentation or slick flyers to hand out or someone waiting at a sign-up table in the back; she simply told her story and said, "I believe we all can do something about this; it shouldn't be this way for these children."

Like most people, Jim and Linda had heard the stats via the nightly news …

- *More than 15 million children under eighteen have been orphaned as a result of AIDS.*
- *Around 11.6 million of these children live in sub-Saharan Africa.*
- *In countries such as Zambia and Botswana, more than 20 percent of children under seventeen are orphans — and most of them have lost one or both parents to AIDS.*

But that night the class of '85 saw what statistics often fail to provide — a face and a name for each of those three young girls. Jim and Linda later thanked Becky for her words and introduced themselves to the girls. The girls timidly handed Jim and Linda each a beautiful, hand-painted bookmark with the following inscription printed on the back:

"We can do no great things, only small things with great love."

— Mother Teresa

On the drive home (as she sat tightly clutching the two bookmarks) Linda mentioned how fragile the girls' hands were and began to cry. Jim said, "Yes, I know."

●●●

Sam instinctively reached for the water pitcher to refill Linda's glass. "Tell us more about your adoption thoughts."

"Thanks, Sam. Well, Jim and I have been in contact with Becky. We don't know if it's adoption or some form of sponsorship; some organizations really encourage local sponsorship. Right now, we're trying to educate ourselves as to the overall picture; that's really where it starts. Even then, it's overwhelming. We thought it was just Africa, but it's also Asia. Think of it this way — what if you and Phillip died because of some crazy disease? And Maggie, Kate, Sarah, and Lily were supposed to come live with us, but Jim and I were too poor and old to adequately care for them — so they were separated from one another, each living with a different family, possibly even in a different place. Add to that the reality that the girls would probably have to quit school and find work doing something to help contribute to the new household; they might have to do manual labor, beg ... or worse. And what if everyone, including their new households, kept them at arm's length because of the stigma associated with that crazy disease you contracted? That's really what's going on."

"The children are growing up without fathers ..." Jim struggled to complete his sentence. "We're getting older, but we'd really like to try. Older couples can have an easier time at international adoption as opposed to domestic. Somehow, we want to be a part of the story of the orphans."

"Sam and I believe you would be a godsend to a child; we always have," Phillip assured with a gentle squeeze of his friend's shoulder. Jim smiled and turned his attention to Sam.

"But enough about us. Sam, Linda and I have been worried about you. You seem, well … distracted lately." Jim laughed, "Like right now!"

Sam looked up from her coffee mug and responded, "It's the funniest thing, Jim, nothing is really wrong, in fact things are … just fine … and that's the problem! 'Just fine' doesn't seem good enough anymore. I'm wondering if I'm missing something … if there might be … more." Sam was uncomfortably aware of the words as they came out.

Phillip looked Sam's way. Linda caught it and inquired, "Alright, what's that all about?"

Phillip conceded. "Sam and I have talked over the whole *'isn't there more?'* mind-set on more than one occasion and we're in agreement … too often it seems like successful people — people blessed with the job, the home, the cars, the kids — are the ones looking for 'more,' grasping for the next thing, as if *who we are* and *what we have*, what *is* … isn't enough. It sounds a little selfish, self-absorbed."

Linda quickly replied, "But what if the 'more' isn't about us at all. What if the 'more' is about turning from 'success' to 'significance' or, better yet, from 'success' to 'servant,' from 'us' to 'them'? Pastor Jordan said something the other day that really made us think; he even used the *'isn't there more?'* phrase. I'll botch the quote, but here goes: 'It's not that what *is* is not enough; it's that what *is* has been disarranged and is crying out to be put in place.' He said the 'more' we're longing for is already all around us, we're just not aware. We're just not looking for the right 'more.'"

"What are you talking about, Linda?" Phillip asked.

"Maybe it's best if I give you an example from our life. Pastor Jordan asked Jim and me to consider helping with the Soup Kitchen ministry. We've thought about it and have decided to do it. We feel it's much like the situation with the orphans; they've been there all along, we just didn't see them. Maybe helping with the food ministry is another way to start seeing what *is* right here around us. To start finding something 'more.'"

Jim laced his hands together, held them above the table, and wiggled his fingers. "The way I see it, all these things are interconnected. The HIV/AIDS epidemic leaves orphans and widows struggling with poverty and hunger and discrimination ... all these completely overwhelming world issues bleed into one another; they need to be reconciled."

Phillip had always liked that last word. "His will being done on earth as in heaven, like the sermon last week?"

"Exactly," Jim said. "We can't do everything, but we can do something." Jim wiggled his fingers again. "And maybe, just maybe that one something will turn into a bunch of somethings that will make a huge difference. We just feel it's time to start. Right, Linda?"

"Yes. Just having these conversations and being invited to be a part of the Soup Kitchen, it's making us feel really alive. Not that we haven't been, but, I don't know, maybe we haven't been fully alive." Linda chuckled to herself. "I hadn't thought about it, but half-alive is the same thing as half-dead."

Sam seemed lost in thought. Linda noticed.

"We haven't forgotten about you, Samantha Dobbins." Linda continued, "Pastor Jordan said he really needed three new people. Banking-numbers man that he is, Jim figured that the two of us plus one more makes three. We'd like for you to consider joining us." As soon as Linda finished the sentence, their waitress arrived. "Ah, great, our food is here."

The young lady carefully placed each entrée in front of the appropriate person, Sam being the last served. "Please be careful, the plates are hot. May I bring you anything else?"

Sam's reaction was almost automatic: "No thank you, we're fine."

●●●

As soon as the waitress walked away, Phillip jumped back in. "I'm thrilled you're considering adoption and I think you'll be an asset to the Soup Kitchen; but these are life-changing movements. I guess I'm just used to the two of you moving slow and easy; it feels fast."

Jim's response was grave: "Do you know what happens during slow and easy, Phillip? Children die. They don't have that time luxury. I hear your concern for us, I really do, but there is an urgency to these crises — we have to start doing something now. Linda and I have talked around getting involved for awhile, but we kept playing the contingency game: *we'll wait until* _____ …

you fill in the blank! But we've realized we'll never have enough time or money or even the purest of motives. You remember the scene from *It's a Wonderful Life* where old Mr. Potter wants the people in town to wait and save their money before there's even a chance of them having a decent home? Then our hero George Bailey says, 'Wait? Wait for what? Until their children leave them or they're old and broken down….' It's the same here, Phillip. Those children can't wait and we don't want to anymore either."

●●●

The parking lot good-byes consisted of the usual lingering hugs and handshakes. As the Fairchilds walked away, Sam wished she and Phillip hadn't come in separate cars; it would be nice to talk on the way home. Phillip squeezed her hand three times — I.love.you. — and said, "I'll be right behind you. See you at home."

As a child, Sam's parents had taught her to pray. She could still hear her mother's voice: "Just talk to him, Samantha. He's always listening. And call him by his name." Her father's contribution to the instruction was, "Pray with your eyes open, Sam. Trust me." Samantha Dobbins had naturally put away some childhood things when she became a woman, but her approach to prayer had never wavered. It was a gift she passed to her own daughters as well.

Sam put the Trooper into first gear and started home, eyes-wide-open. "Jesus, I really love Thursdays with Jim and Linda. Thank you. I don't quite know what to think about the Soup

Kitchen ... I can usually smell guilt and I didn't sense anything tonight except sincerity, even possibility. At the same time, it still frustrated me a little and I don't like that, but it did. I know it's an evil generation that seeks for a sign, but I'm not a generation ... I'm me and I would love ... I'd love some kind of sign. I don't know how else to say ..."

Sam didn't make it to the end of her prayer because of what she saw parked on the side of the road up ahead — the beater pickup from earlier in the day, *I Brake for No Apparent Reason* bumper sticker and all. This time, however, the hood was raised and steam was rising from the edges. Sam felt her heart rise up in her throat. She slowed the Trooper, put on her blinker to alert Phillip, and pulled in behind the pickup. She opened her door and sat for a moment, giving Phillip time to walk up. "I hope the next time I have car trouble, I get a Good Samaritan as pretty as you." She smiled and took his hand. "Just please come with me, okay?" And hand in hand they walked toward the truck.

Sam's mother used to say, "The Lord works in mysterious ways." And her father would always complement with, "Yes, and then sometimes it's as obvious as the wind in Kansas." Sam literally had no idea what was up ahead but she did notice the gentlest of breezes against her skin. If she didn't know better, she might think it a sign.

●●●

Luci Dillard's check-engine light had been on three days shy of one year, exactly the amount of time since Kurt's death. Sergeant First Class Kurt Dillard was killed when his Humvee hit a roadside bomb in Ramadi, Iraq. It was his third tour of duty and they'd hoped his last. It was. She played the strong military widow at the graveside, but when the gloved officer presented a folded flag, Luci finally broke down. Her breakdown was followed by others: washer/dryer, refrigerator, computer, and now the pickup. She was trying to be present for the kids and give some semblance of coping for anyone who cared to look, but inside she was half-dead.

"Damn, damn, damn." She raised the hood of the truck and watched steam rise off the engine. "God … Kurt, I …" Her wish was stopped midsentence by someone clearing their throat.

●●●

Sam had no idea who the pickup's driver might be; best guess, an older man. She steadied herself and stepped toward the front of the truck. "Ahem. Excuse me, is there any way we can help you?" Sam and Phillip were greeted by fallen shoulders in a faded army jacket; a young woman's eyes raised to meet theirs. For a moment they just looked at one another. Sam looked for a cell phone in the woman's hands, but saw nothing.

Sam spoke into the silence. "I'm Sam and this is my husband Phillip. We'd be happy to help you if we can." Phillip immediately started poking around under the hood. He had no idea what he was doing, but sometimes that's what men do.

The young woman spoke directly to Sam. "Thanks, but I'll figure it out." Her voice and expression were flat, no emotion. "You're nice to stop, but I'll be fine." Sam cringed at that last word.

Phillip gave his non-mechanic analysis: "I'm afraid you're going to need a wrecker."

Sam said, "Look, it's getting late. At least let us call someone for you or let me drive you home." Usually Sam would see her daughters or Phillip in the face of the person needing help and think something like, *If this were Maggie, I'd sure want someone to help her.* But this moment surprised Sam; the face she kept seeing was her own. Her words came out — "Please, let me help you" — but there was a strange sense in Sam of "Please, won't you help me?"

The young woman started to reach her hand toward the truck, but then withdrew it. "Okay, I'll take you up on that ride. It's not very far."

Sam took a few steps back and made a half-turn, opening the route to her Trooper.

"Thank you," the young woman said.

Sam smiled. "You're welcome … I didn't get your name."

"It's Luci … with an 'i'."

"You're welcome, Luci."

Phillip offered to wait for a wrecker but Luci assured him she would take care of it tomorrow. He looked at Sam and she nodded *let it be*. As Luci walked from her pickup, Phillip sidled up to Sam and whispered, "You sure you'll be alright? I'm happy to ride along if you want."

"I'll be okay," Sam assured. "Go on home so Elly can leave. Get the girls ready for bed. I'll call if I need you."

Phillip raised the volume enough so Luci could hear. "Alright then, ladies. Sam, see you at home. Luci, you're in good hands."

Sam quickly moved to the passenger side of her Trooper. "Luci, give me a moment. I just need to make room for you." Sam quickly moved stacks of papers and books from the front seat to the back. As she did, the weight of her last statement lingered on her mind: "to make room." She couldn't help but think of one of the many things she loved about Santa Fe: the annual tradition of La Posada, or "the Inn." For nine days leading up to Christmas, characters reenact Mary and Joseph's journey of rejection from place to place with the repeated refrain of "no room." The days culminate on Christmas Eve with a feast and piñatas; finally, a place is found for Christ to be born. "Alright, Luci. There you go."

Phillip waited for Sam and Luci to pull away before he started his car. As he eased forward he noticed the blue bumper sticker. He laughed a moment and then paused, wondering just where Sam was headed. "Lord, have mercy on those two. Amen."

Luci gave Sam an address and commentary: "If you hit all the green lights, it will take just a few minutes." Her attention was then drawn to the photo taped to Sam's console. "Your family?"

"Yes. Phillip you met and those are our girls."

"Looks complete," Luci added. "They're beautiful."

"Thank you." Sam initially didn't feel the need to fill the space with talking, but Luci had started, so she decided to follow. As Luci had pointed to the photo, Sam noticed a wedding ring. "Do you have children?"

"My boys are seven and eight. My dad got laid off, so my parents have been living with us. The boys like having them around."

Sam didn't always like this about herself, but she was a bloodhound when it came to language, what people said and what they didn't, choices of particles of speech. Her mind picked up the scent of Luci's description of "my" boys, not "ours." She continued with caution. "Phillip's a good dad. I'm not sure how he does it in a house full of females, but he does. The girls cherish him; so do I."

The inside of the Trooper grew quiet. "It's faster if you take a left at the next light." Then Luci made it easy on her. "I still wear the ring, but he's gone. Kurt was killed in Iraq a year ago. He was a good dad too."

Sam couldn't help but notice the emptiness in Luci's voice. She spoke as one still in shock, like someone half-dead. "How long were you married?"

Luci's voice rose slightly. "Not long enough."

"Luci, I'm sorry." And those three words seemed enough for both of them, for now.

＊＊＊

Across town, Jordan Ross was putting the finishing touches on his message for Sunday. For many in his congregation the phrase *Sunday's comin'* held hope and promise, resurrection. For Jordan, it held a reminder that the people would show up wanting to be fed, consumers one and all. He didn't rail against the consumer mind-set like some of his peers. He believed we're all consuming something, the question is *what*. Sunday was coming and he wanted to make sure he'd prepared well so his proclamation would complement the main course— communion. But there was trouble in the kitchen of his mind.

The text for Sunday was the story of the Good Samaritan. It would be a familiar passage to most of the people. And that's what worried Jordan. Earlier in the week he had written down the phrase *familiarity breeds contempt*. He believed it true about this passage. His fear was that he would open his Bible, read the text, and the people would close their minds and smile and nod and later shake his hand and say, "Great message today."

"A man was going down from Jerusalem to Jericho, when he fell into the hands of robbers. They stripped him of his clothes, beat him and went away, leaving him half dead ..."

As he chewed on the text in his mind throughout the week, the two-word sandwich *half-dead* proved tough as gristle. He typed the eight letters in his search engine and discovered that, according to one website, people who are half-dead are "neither alive nor dead, and as such, fall into the classification of either inanimate objects or cats." He laughed until he cried on that one, but knew there were more than a few cat lovers in the congregation. Familiarity might breed contempt, but jabs at a pet could cost you your job.

Half-dead. It seemed to describe most of the people he knew, in his congregation or not; some days, even himself. Not dead, because then you'd be dead and well, dead is dead. But at the same time, not alive, at least not the fully alive kind of alive made popular by evangelical superstar authors who milked John 10:10 for all it's worth. No, *half-dead*, quite possibly a condition worse than the other two. He couldn't say that anyone had ever responded with those two words when he asked how they were doing. Plenty would answer with *fine* or *alright*, but those were words you might easily hear from an inanimate object. Or maybe a cat.

His method of sermon preparation was to immerse himself in the text early in the week and then look and listen the rest of the week for the verses to incarnate themselves in everyday life. As he continued grinding *half-dead* through that daily process, he eventually spit out the word *exhaustion*: "Ah, now there's a word to consider." He remembered an evening several months ago. Phillip Dobbins had invited him to hear a popular poet speak; the topic for the night was "Magnificence."

The highlight of the evening for Jordan was the poet's recollection of a conversation he'd had with a man of well-known monkish proportions. He'd asked the Brother to tell him the antidote for exhaustion; the Brother's answer had stunned the poet, as it did Jordan:

"The antidote is not rest; it's wholeheartedness. *Half-anything* will eventually kill you."

Sunday was comin', but he still had two days to hone his thoughts. Friday was his usual day off and he planned to hike a little in the morning and run errands in the afternoon. Saturday was Grace's twice-a-month Soup Kitchen; he would need to be on hand to guide Jim and Linda Fairchild through their first experience. So far, those Saturdays were always brimming with trouble, but it was the right kind of trouble.

●●●

Finished with his work for the day, Jordan Ross did one final check of his email and noticed an "unread" in his inbox. He debated about opening something just before heading to bed, but the flesh was weak. A friend from the University of Portland sent him an overview of the Ecumenical Ministries of Oregon's 40th Annual Collins Lecture. The honored speaker for the event was Archbishop Desmond Tutu; he gave Jordan his good-night story:

One of the most powerful examples of the transformative power of truth and reconciliation was Tutu's recounting of the death of Amy Biehl, a Stanford University student on a Fulbright Scholarship in Cape Town during the struggle against apartheid. Ironically, she was stabbed to death by four young antiapartheid fighters, who saw only the color of her skin.

In 1998, Biehl's killers were pardoned by the Truth and Reconciliation Commission (a decision her family endorsed) and released from prison after serving only four years. At the amnesty hearings, Amy's parents shook hands with their daughter's killers. Amy's father, Peter Biehl, addressed the Commission saying, "The most important vehicle of reconciliation is open and honest dialogue.... We are here to reconcile a human life which was taken without an opportunity for dialogue. When we are finished with this process we must move forward with linked arms."

Tutu called the Biehls' reaction "mind blowing." Two of Amy Biehl's killers were employed by her parents at a foundation they established in Amy's name; the work continues to this day to eradicate poverty in the slums of Cape Town. "Mahatma Gandhi was right," said the archbishop, "where the maxim 'an eye for an eye' is employed, soon everyone will be blind."

● ● ●

Isabel had walked through the historic town square that evening. She would watch people and try to imagine what it would be like to be them, to live their lives instead of her own. As she passed a restaurant, two couples were sitting outside at a table, talking like people who were very familiar with one another, like good friends. Isabel stopped for a moment and stared. To her eyes, the men and women looked like those families she occasionally watched on television; not the "new season" offerings, but the older sitcoms like *Eight Is Enough*, shows where people seemed to care for each other and everything always worked out. That's what she saw in the couples as they laughed and spoke to each other.

Isabel could usually place herself in another's life with ease, but this was difficult; it was almost beyond her imaginings to ever have the love of a husband. There had been a number of men in her life, but they were only interested in a brief bit of time, nothing like months or years or a lifetime. But there was one when she was barely twenty; his name was Paul. He told her he loved her and she had believed him, although she wasn't certain what the word truly meant. They stole moments together when they could and shared dreams of running away from it all. Paul had strong arms, like the boy who had saved her that night so long ago. Being with him made Isabel happy. But when he would leave, voices deep inside assured her it would not last. Still, she tried to hope.

There was a woman who owned Isabel; at least she always told her, "You're mine." This woman found out about Paul. It wasn't long afterward that he told Isabel he did not love her anymore: "Don't cry. You're too pretty to cry." Isabel did not cry, although she wanted to.

She had the same feeling watching the couples at the restaurant. She wanted to cry because their lives were so far from her own, but she couldn't. She wondered sometimes if she'd forgotten how. If the scene at the restaurant had been a television sitcom it would have been called *Four Is Enough*. Isabel's life had taught her that *One Is Enough* … but she did wish, from time to time, there was another one. That would make *two*.

2

"Where there's desolation and heartbreak," he said, "there's beauty and magic."

Harry Middleton,
The Earth Is Enough

Phillip walked the house one last time before going to bed. It was ritual. He wanted to make sure doors were locked and lights were off, but mainly to make sure the four girls in two bedrooms were safe and sound. They were. Both rooms fell asleep to music, so Phillip clicked off the radios. The oldest, Maggie and Kate, were spreading their own musical wings, drifting off to three brothers named Jonas. The twins, however, had stumbled upon the local easy-listening station one night and demanded it ever since. Many nights Phillip would sit on the floor between their twin beds until Mathis and Sinatra crooned them to sleep.

He had a trip coming up in a month; it would be two weeks away, writing a feature story for the magazine. Only fourteen days, but he was already missing his nighttime ritual. He was still humming "Wee Small Hours of the Morning" as he slipped into bed beside Sam. "You've been rather quiet since you got home. Do you want to talk about Luci?"

"Phillip, I saw that white pickup several times today. It was strange, like I couldn't get away from it. So when I saw it tonight, I really had no choice; I couldn't pass on by."

"Sam, you know you've always got a choice."

"It wasn't like I was being forced or anything, Phillip. It was more like one last chance if I wanted it. In some ways it felt like Jim and Linda's invitation at dinner, like …"

"Like a chance for something *more*?"

"I wasn't going to use that word, but yes, that's exactly how it felt." She smiled and sat up cross-legged. "The young woman I took home tonight — Luci? She's a widow, her husband was killed in Iraq. Her two boys are about the age of Lily and Sarah … Phillip, if I were in her shoes, I don't know if I could do it. I really don't."

Phillip did not hear pity in Sam's voice, so he probed deeper. "You seem drawn to her."

"She's so alone. You saw it in her eyes, didn't you? I mean, look at me, I'm surrounded by you and good friends and church and the school; I've got so many soft places to fall. But I didn't sense that in Luci's life. It's just her and the ground … and the ground at her feet these days is hard. I drove away wanting so much to help her."

"Sam, you did. I didn't see any other cars stopped to help her out. But you did. What she needed in that moment was a ride home; you provided that, right?"

Sam straightened her legs and wiggled her toes. "Yes, I did, but I just touched the surface."

"Touch … the deadliest enemy of convention." Phillip spoke the words with a poet's eye. "That's where it begins, Sam. Touch. It's a start, a good one. How did you leave things with Luci?"

"I asked if I might call her and see if there was any way we could help with the truck. She waffled a minute and then said yes. We exchanged phone numbers, she sidestepped some toys in the front yard, and then she was gone. She never looked back. Phillip, I'd like to invite her and the boys over for dinner tomorrow night. We had planned to have Elly over anyway, so what's three more people?"

Phillip was a little surprised. "You're serious, aren't you?"

"Yes. C'mon, I'll let you try out your polenta recipe." Sam batted her eyes at her husband of fifteen years, something that still made him grin.

"Alright. You are a sly one, Samantha Dobbins. Call her and see if they can come. I'm guessing they'll need a ride." Phillip paused for a few seconds, then added, "I sure wish you could go with me next month." The truth was, Sam did too.

The magazine Phillip wrote for was planning a feature article on clean water initiatives. They had several writing teams reporting stateside efforts, but wanted at least one team to go abroad, cover the global perspective. The managing editor knew how to tempt Phillip: "If the article goes well, there could be a book in there somewhere; that's often the way these things happen. Besides, you'd be covering a group of Christian workers. We need someone who will report accurately what's going on, but also show a little mercy." The editor's words came with a wink.

Phillip wouldn't balk at a book deal and the money wasn't bad, but he accepted the assignment primarily because he was interested in Christianity's current infatuation with all things "justice." He had seen T-shirts on some of Sam's students that read SEEK JUSTICE. Something about it didn't sit well with him. He had voiced his feeling to Jordan Ross one Sunday and the young pastor's remark both clarified and challenged.

"Phillip, justice is desperately needed in our world. But I believe it has to come from the right place. You're a smart guy; go read Micah 6:8 again and look for the heartbeat of the verse."

"And what does the LORD require of you? To act justly and to love mercy and to walk humbly with your God."
—Micah 6:8

Phillip received a 3 x 5 postcard a few days later with the church's return address. It was blank except for these lines: *Only by loving mercy can justice worth a God's blood be done to the uttermost.*

* * *

Phillip had been doing his homework for the trip, trying to get a feel for some of the work that was going on. He knew the phrase "clean water is life," but clean water efforts in the U.S. were broadly geared, encompassing everything from safe places to swim to protecting certain species of fish. Outside the U.S., however, clean water meant something less wide.

At any given time, half of the world's hospital beds are occupied by patients suffering from a water-related disease. Nearly 90 percent of all diseases in the world are caused by unsafe drinking water, inadequate sanitation, and poor hygiene. Every year there are 4 billion cases of diarrhea as a direct result of drinking contaminated water; this results in more than 2.2 million deaths each year — the equivalent of twenty jumbo jets crashing every day. The weakest members of communities are the most vulnerable; every day water-related diseases claim the lives of 5,000 children under the age of five. That's roughly one every fifteen seconds.

Phillip's team would be heading to Uganda, a country with a recorded population of between 27 and 30 million people, with numbers possibly reaching 50 million people by the year 2025. Over 100,000 children worldwide die every day from the lack of clean drinking water; many of these children are in places like the rural areas of Uganda.

A local physician from Grace Church had traveled a number of times to Uganda and other African locales on short-term mission endeavors. Phillip had visited with him several times and once asked, "What do you think of when I say 'clean drinking water'?" The doctor's answer held no wiggle room: "In places like Uganda? Phillip, it's life or death. It is the number-one way to effectively impact health care."

Phillip would be journaling the team's goal of constructing a water-harvesting tank in the village of Kagoma. Water would be collected from the roof of a church building and then channeled to an underground cement tank capable of holding up to 50 kiloliters of water. If met, this goal could serve about 150 homes in the village with clean water for drinking, cooking, and washing clothes. Phillip felt certain some of those homes would have little girls in them, girls like the four sleeping soundly across the hall, who were never bothered by questions of water.

●●●

"I wish I could go with you too, Phillip, but I can't. This time it's about you," Sam said.

She was baiting him and he knew it. "Oh, so sometimes it is about me?" Phillip put his hands behind his head and beamed so she couldn't miss it.

"Sometimes it's about the poet. Not always, but sometimes. Now kiss me and go to sleep. And thank you for saying yes to Luci."

●●●

As was his custom, Phillip was asleep minutes after the lights went out. But not Sam. She could not get an image out of her mind — Luci's shoes, or rather her boots. Sam had noticed them when Luci first sat down beside her — big black cowboy boots, easily two to three sizes too large for the slender legs above them. Sam spied them again when Luci got out and navigated the toys in the yard. The military widow didn't so much raise her feet as slide them, as if she were making sure something didn't fall away. Sam wasn't a betting woman, but she was willing to wager the boots belonged to the man who no longer slept beside Luci at night.

"Jesus, have mercy on Luci and her boys," Sam whispered. "Mercy on us all. Amen."

By the closed bedroom door, Luci knew her parents had gone on to bed; the boys had no doubt worn them out. She was thankful and not so thankful for their presence. Someone to help with the boys, especially when she had to work late or extra shifts, was a godsend. But the house was small to begin with; privacy was rare. And then there was the unspoken awkwardness.

After Kurt's death a silent distance had grown between them she couldn't seem to cover. Her parents had been childhood sweethearts, recently celebrating forty years of marriage; they'd never been without the other. It was almost as if they no longer shared a common language with their daughter; they spoke as one while she spoke alone. Little did she know how much her loss terrified her father and mother; Kurt's death had revealed that thieves and robbers were at large in their sheltered world.

Luci placed her palms on Kurt Jr.'s and David's sleeping chests. It was ritual, or at least it was now; Kurt had performed it in the past. They were both in the same bed, again, each facing the opposite direction. Kurt Jr. and David had been sleeping like this ever since the funeral. The picture of her sleeping boys was that of Siamese twins, joined at the shoulders by too much sadness too soon. Early on she had wondered if them sleeping together was right, but she had come to the point where she believed it was good.

The lamp on their nightstand shone on the open book, as if holding the place last read. Maybe her mother had read a few pages to the boys before they had fallen asleep. Kurt's sister had sent the book not long after he died — *The Velveteen Rabbit* by Margery Williams. Luci was only vaguely familiar with the story of the rabbit that asked, "What does it mean to be real?" They had read the story together many times in the last year. She wasn't sure the boys could understand everything on the pages, but she believed they knew what it was about. Luci raised the book and eyed the page:

"Does it hurt?" asked the Rabbit.

"Sometimes," said the Skin Horse, for he was always truthful …

"You're right, Skin Horse," Luci whispered. "Sometimes it hurts." Luci headed to her darkened bedroom and sat on the edge of the bed. The moon through the blinds shed just enough light to reveal the Serenity Prayer's framed conclusion on the wall:

> … That I may be reasonably happy in this life
> and supremely happy with Him
> Forever in the next.
> Amen.

This life only gets reasonably happy? she voicelessly asked the moon.

She easily slipped out of Kurt's boots and sunk back into the bed and thought about her broken-down pickup and her well-intentioned parents and the fatherless boys sleeping across the hall and some woman named Sam who stopped and seemed to care. She let out an involuntary sob, reached over and pulled Kurt's pillow tight against her body, and drifted off to sleep.

Luci dreamed that night of the things most people don't bother to find out about and really don't want to know. Like the military instructor who told her she was surprised Luci wasn't prepared for the possibility of Kurt dying. Or fending off inappropriate sexual advances from other officers, some of them Kurt's close friends. Or the relatives wanting to borrow money from the insurance payment, what little there was. And a strange couple, friends of her parents, who assured her Kurt's death was a part of God's plan, that God wouldn't put more on her than she could bear.

Early on, after Kurt died, she let the stuff of those memories roll off her; people just didn't know better, they weren't thinking. But it was becoming too much. People *should* know better, they *should* be thinking, at least trying. It felt like everyone just wanted her to work through the grief, achieve something called closure, and pick up where she left off. Happy, smiling people, especially couples, are what America wanted to see; there was no demand for weepy war widows.

As recently as two weeks ago, Luci's girlfriends took her out to eat for her birthday. As they entered the restaurant, a uniformed officer with family in tow walked out and that was that. Luci lost it, right there in the crowded entryway. Her friends and even the hostess tried to console her, but it was no use. She apologized profusely and insisted on driving herself home. She fumbled with her keys out at the pickup and dropped her purse. Everything spilled at her boots except a lipstick she saw roll under the truck.

Luci knelt to try to gather herself and her things. The touch on her shoulder was light, courteous, beckoning her to stand. The voice was comfortable: "Hey, this rolled to the other side. They don't give lipstick away these days, do they?" Luci found it hard to focus through her tears. "Shucks, some days I have to go around my elbow to get to my thumb too. Listen, whatever it is, go slow. Just go slow."

Luci thought it was the nicest thing anyone had done for her in a long, long time.

●●●

It was too late to be out for a casual drive, yet Jim and Linda Fairchild were doing just that. In their conversations with Pastor Ross about the Soup Kitchen ministry, he had challenged them to prep themselves by driving the streets some night, late, and pay attention to what they saw.

"The night is its own world, full of sights and sounds and smells we never experience in the light of day. Give yourself time to adjust though; it takes a little while to befriend the night. Map out a route and drive it."

"Wouldn't it be better if we walked rather than drove?" Linda wondered. "I mean, that way we would be closer to things or people."

Pastor Ross smiled. "Maybe. But start out by driving, slow.

And so the banker and his wife rolled down the windows and for over an hour they crept along the streets of Santa Fe that late Thursday almost Friday.

They saw a handful of kids entering a convenience store, a semi driver artfully backing up to a loading dock, a waitress wiping down tables through the IHOP window, an old white pickup on the roadside with the hood raised, and a young woman walking hand in hand with a small boy. Finally, the pre-scribed route almost complete, Jim slowed in the left turn lane that would carry them back toward home. It was a left turn they both took countless times each week, but neither could remember ever seeing the wooden bench on the corner.

What drew their attention there in the first place was the slumped figure that stood as they turned. The shadowy charac-ter hobbled to the edge of the curb, raised both arms, and gave the Fairchilds the bird, one on each hand. Through their open windows they heard his howl: "F bombs" launched at them … at the night … at the world in general.

Jim and Linda had been flipped off before in traffic, but never in such dramatic fashion. This man played the scene like some Shakespearean actor. Linda turned to watch through the back glass and Jim focused on the rearview mirror; the figure held his pose until fading from their view.

Jim pulled in their driveway and broke the silence. "Well, that was quite a colorful finale to our late-night drive."

"Jim, did you notice how he lingered? It was almost like he was trying to scare us off, but make sure we saw him at the same time."

Jim paused to consider his choice of words. Then with that mischievous smile that Linda knew all too well, he replied,

"You know, if I ever decide to do a two-handed-dramatic-gutsy screw 'em, I want to do it like that guy."

Linda sighed. "Well, if you do, you'll be on your own." She thought a moment and then added, "But you know, if you think about it, maybe the real profane thing is not what that man is saying but the way he may be living his everyday life. I know that I don't really ever want to use language like that, but surely there's something deeper there than vowels and consonants. I sound like Phillip, don't I? He's always saying 'the letters C-O-W don't give milk.'"

Jim grinned. "Well, I don't know about that, but if we're going to really try to make some kind of a difference, we can't let the first offense shut us down."

He watched until their car faded from view, muttering another obscenity or two as he walked back to the bench. The wooden frame would not be the most comfortable place to sleep, but for a few hours, it would be the safest place on the street. "Always trying to get old Louis, aren't they, Jesus H.? But I won't let 'em. Maybe someday, but not yet."

As a young boy Louis heard his father say "Jesus H. Christ" countless times a day. His father's familiar blasphemy was always tempered by the King James hidden in his mother's heart; she wove Scripture into every sentence she spoke. These days, Louis preferred to live in the past and so to honor his father and mother, he addressed the Lord as Jesus H., but always with his mother's reverence.

He couldn't exactly remember how long he'd been in Santa Fe; it didn't matter anyway. He liked it here, most days that is, but not today. He was glad to see this day end. "Those boys shouldn't've kicked me, Jesus H. Why would anybody need to kick Louis?" The sixty-two-year-old man groaned as he stretched the length of the bench, then turned several times to search for a position that might offer some rest. "Why would anybody kick Louis?"

●●●

Louis couldn't answer that question, but there are answers. Between 1999 and 2007, over 770 violent acts against homeless individuals were documented by advocacy organizations. These attacks ranged from beatings with golf clubs to setting a man on fire while sleeping. Victims have included men and women, veterans, children as young as four, teenagers, and elders. During that same time period, more fatal attacks were documented against homeless individuals than in all legally recognized hate crime categories combined.

The stories of hate, stories like Louis's, are almost overwhelming:

A fifty-three-year-old man named Michael was beaten to death with sticks and logs by a group of teenagers who admitted it was "just for fun." The autopsy report indicated death due to blunt-force trauma to the head and body, along with a fractured skull, broken ribs, badly injured legs, and defensive wounds on his hands.

A fifty-one-year-old man named William was kicked, punched, and finally bludgeoned to death by two New York City teenagers.

The attack took place in a churchyard. The teens left and William summoned enough strength to crawl to the church steps, where his strength and his life ended.

A piece of the answer lies in the virtually invisible nature of the homeless: no permanent address, essentially no possessions, usually no identification, and unfortunately no one to wonder why they didn't come home that night. Violent crimes against the homeless happen because the homeless are perceived to have no value, no worth; they are outside the circle of societal protection and justice. In other words, tragically vulnerable.

"Why would anybody kick Louis?" Louis guessed the answer to be *because they can.*

●●●

The boys had happened upon Louis early Thursday morning. He had fallen asleep the night before against an adobe wall surrounding the casita downtown. The pizza delivery boy left his car for only a moment, but that was long enough for Louis to open the passenger side door and take the two large boxes. Louis shuffled two or three blocks and discovered the hidden portion of the wall — a good place to hide and eat and sleep.

He had fallen asleep full, satisfied. He awoke in terror, a coat wrapped around his head, his stomach being kicked repeatedly. Louis screamed, "Jesus H.!" And for some reason, maybe in answer to his cry, the kicking stopped and the coat was pulled from his head. A boy's voice said "Leave it," and then they were gone.

Louis finally found an angle on the bench where the pain in his ribs eased. As his breathing slowed, memory rose in the sound of his mother's voice at bedtime. "Green and still, Louis … green and still." The words brought warmth to his face; they were his mother's shorthand for the 23rd Psalm. "The only two adjectives King David chose." And so in short breaths, Louis whispered alongside his mother's voice:

The LORD … maketh me to lie down in green pastures … beside the still waters.

"I'm laying down now, Jesus H."

Yea, though I walk … Thou art with me … in the presence of mine enemies …

"Getting tired of walking everywhere. Getting tired of bad people."

Surely goodness and mercy shall follow me all the days of my life …

"They shouldn't've kicked Louis. Mercy on Louis tonight. Amen."

●●●

Louis used to be what social service agencies define as homeless — a person lacking "a fixed, regular, and adequate nighttime residence." But now he was among the chronic homeless — "an unaccompanied homeless individual with a disabling condition (e.g., substance abuse, serious mental illness, developmental disability, or chronic physical illness) who has either been continuously homeless for a year or more, or has had at least four episodes of homelessness in the past three years."

Although the stats were lost on a man like Louis, the National Law Center on Homelessness and Poverty estimates between 2.3 and 3.5 million Americans experience homelessness. A study in 2007 by the National Alliance to End Homelessness indicated Alaska, California, Colorado, Hawaii, Idaho, Nevada, Oregon, Rhode Island, Washington State, and Washington, D.C. as having the highest rates of homelessness. And the U.S. Interagency Council on Homelessness says that while most homeless are unaccompanied adults, like Louis, the number of homeless families is growing:

- *66 percent are single adults, and of these, three-quarters are men;*
- *11 percent are parents with children, 84 percent of whom are single women;*
- *23 percent are children under 18 with a parent, 42 percent of those are under five years of age.*

There are the homeless that look like Louis and fit the stereotypes, and then there are the homeless that don't. The latter is growing larger every day.

●●●

Homelessness had never been an issue for Elly; there was always someone around — parents or a brother or a roommate. Elly's current roommate, Kris, fell asleep to the radio most nights. At first it drove Elly batty, but she got used to it. Elly was just slightly awake; Kris was already snoring. The public station was replaying an interview with historian/sociologist Rodney Stark; he had spoken recently at the college. It was obvious the reporter was asking preset questions, but they were still good questions.

Reporter: Why did the Christian movement grow so rapidly in the first few centuries after Jesus' crucifixion? His followers were a small band of social outcasts, ragtags at best. What is to be credited for their evolution into such a global force?

Stark: The growth surge of Christianity was rooted in the response of early Christians to a wave of great pandemics. At least two plagues wracked the developing world in the first three centuries after the death of Christ. During that time, Christians did something no one else did.

Reporter: And what was that?

Stark: It sounds simple, but they stayed. They helped. And many gave their lives in doing so. In my book, *The Rise of Christianity*, I refer to a letter written by Dionysius, the bishop of Alexandria. He describes how early Christians responded to a deadly plague that killed an estimated five thousand people a day in the Roman Empire sometime around AD 260: "Most of our brother Christians showed unbounded love and loyalty, never sparing themselves and thinking only of one another. Heedless of danger, they took charge of the sick, attending to

their every need and ministering to them in Christ ...
they were infected by others with the disease, drawing
on themselves the sickness of the neighbors and cheer-
fully accepting their pains. Many, in nursing and curing
others, transferred their death to themselves and died
in their stead ..."

Elly reached over, switched off the radio, and lay still. Stark's
words hung in the air. The girl from Alabama wondered if she
could have done as much in AD 260; she wanted to think so.
Everyone who knew Elly believed her constitution to be of the
"steel magnolia" variety. But that wasn't always the case, like
two weeks ago.

She simply picked up a runaway tube of lipstick and
returned it to the owner. But the owner's eyes betrayed a fra-
gility Elly hadn't seen lately. As she handed the lipstick back,
the woman received it with both hands, as if it were a robin's
egg or a long lost coin. Her hands brushed against Elly's only
for a moment, but Elly felt a transfer just the same; more was
exchanged than lipstick.

She couldn't remember exactly what her parting words
were, something like "Bless your heart ... just go slow." The
memory embarrassed Elly now: *What a shallow thing to say to
someone so obviously in pain.*

Elly felt a tear stream down her cheek. Stark's words still lingered: "Heedless of danger ... they were infected by others."
She hadn't thought to heed the danger of pausing to pick up a
lipstick — it seemed so safe, but now it was too late.

She wiped the tear and remembered her latest book club read — *Eat, Pray, Love*. She was in no way smitten with it but, like most things, there were places worthy of an asterisk or underline if you paid attention. One such paragraph contained the phrase *L'ho provato sulla mia pelle* — "I have experienced that on my own skin." The country of origin was Italy; the context for the phrase was empathy. Elly had underlined the paragraph. She had no idea if she knew exactly what the young woman with the runaway lipstick was going through, but she had been grazed by another's pain in the midst of her usual errands of madness. It was palpable; she had felt it on her own skin.

Many of the people who surrounded Elly believed her to be this sensitive by nature, but she knew better. She was still learning the lesson that started by being Billy's sister. In a move that completely shocked her family's circle of friends, Elly's parents took in a twenty-year-old Cambodian woman named Tevy in 1988. The church her parents attended supported a group of young refugees as they came to the States in search of a better life. Tevy was two months pregnant and Elly's mother and father believed God told them, *Take care of that girl*. And so they did.

All went fairly well until the final month of Tevy's pregnancy, when complications arose that necessitated a C-section and the baby was not breathing at birth. By the time the doctors revived him, the newborn had been without oxygen for almost two minutes; everything from speech to muscle control were forever altered. Tevy died later that day. Elly's mother named the boy Billy because she had been saved at a Billy Graham crusade in Atlanta and had always called it *one of the happiest days of my life.* One year later, Elly was born. She was the first from her mother's body, but in many ways she was the second child.

A special education teacher recognized what he called "gifts" in Billy and convinced Elly's parents to place him in a normal class structure to accelerate his learning. Billy's jerky movement and slurred speech stood out against the conformed tide of grade school. Elly never resented Billy's presence in their lives, but there were days when the ridicule was hard to bear. Billy loved his sister, of that there was no doubt. He would call her name from across a room or down the hall: "Ell-ah-Lee! Ell-ah-Lee!" But even love is some days hard for a sixth grader to bear.

Billy saw people the other kids missed; he always said *he-ll-oh* to the lady in the school cafeteria and waved wildly to the man who mowed the grass at church. And he seemed to understand the people in the nursing home. The youth group at Elly's church would visit once a month and sing old hymns. It was always hard to get Billy to leave.

Rain thrilled him but he was afraid of thunder. Any time the sky boomed during the night, he would call for her: "Ell-ah-Lee! Ell-ah-Lee!" She would go to his bedside and quietly sing his favorite hymn — "Swing Low, Sweet Chariot." He always giggled when she sang the *swing low* part in a really low, raspy voice. Billy always joined her on the last word — *hoh-mme.*

One night Elly asked her father what God was going to do to help Billy in this world. The man from whom she got her dimpled cheeks didn't miss a beat: "He gave him a sister like you, Ell." Just eight little words, but her dad spoke volumes. Elly continued to struggle; it was still challenging having Billy for a brother, but it wasn't hard.

On the day of his fifteenth birthday, Elly and her mother made his favorite meal — macaroni and cheese. On that night, it rained without thunder, not even so much as a low rumble. Billy slept with his window open and the cool night air combined with the rain to give his fragile body pneumonia. Six weeks later, that sweet chariot swung low and took Billy hoh-mme.

Elly had always been drawn to the biblical story of Jacob's wrestling — the Old Testament trickster being wounded by the Lord himself. Jacob limped after that. She believed Billy's death was such a wounding. Elly limped slightly from then on; you couldn't see it, but she could feel it. The limp slowed her down, caused her to pay attention, see people others missed. Elly believed she was not this sensitive by nature, but being Billy's sister had changed all that, all that and more. She had experienced it on her own skin.

●●●

Isabel's mind tended to stay in the past. As she walked late that night with the boy's hand in her own, memories of desire and kindness and regret were stirred.

Once she had known for certain, she had begged the woman to let her keep the child: *Please, please … I'll do anything.* Most men took, but Paul had given something of himself to her; maybe he had loved her after all. She knew in some abstract way there would be suffering in carrying the child, but she had no idea. Several weeks later as she walked through the alleyway behind the old church, she miscarried, passing out next to a rusting dumpster overflowing with garbage.

As she began to drift back into consciousness she had a vague sense of someone lifting her and then carrying her, almost like the boy who had carried her away from her mother's side years before. But this was not a boy. Isabel thought she heard him say "hospital" — she whispered a weak *Please, no.* Again, everything went black.

She opened her eyes to see a man and woman facing away, talking. The man's tone was hushed but clear: "There are no damaged goods when everyone is damaged goods." Isabel found herself in a short bed in the middle of a soft yellow room. The woman turned and gently sat beside her, and offered broth through a straw, as one might nurse an injured bird. "It's okay ..."

"Isabel," Isabel finished the sentence for her.

"You're ... safe here ... Isabel," the woman said. Isabel believed her and quickly returned to sleep.

When Isabel awoke next — more than twenty-four hours later — the house was completely quiet, save for the sound of gentle snoring drifting from down the hall. She hated to leave the yellow room, but the house and the man and the woman were not her life. She tiptoed toward what she guessed was the front of the house. As she turned to pull the front door closed behind her, she could have sworn she heard the woman's voice speak softly from the shadows: "Good-bye, Isabel." Isabel paused, then slipped quickly away.

Her body suffered for weeks after, but she endured. From the outside, it looked as if she had fully recovered, but the scars were there. Isabel guessed it was central to her life to ache.

As the little boy tried to pull away, her mind was jerked back to the present. The child she walked with tonight was not her own. The woman told her to watch him while she visited with a man that evening. The boy was not from her body, but he could have been if things had been different.

There were moments she thought of the kind man, his wife, and the yellow room. Tonight a part of her wished he would not have been so kind, that he would have piled the trash bags on top of her and left her with the garbage. It might have been more merciful.

friday

3

Purity does not lie in a separation from the universe, but in a deeper penetration of it.

Pierre Teilhard
de Chardin

Fridays were opportunities for Jordan Ross to get "out of the way." He had observed these sabbaths ever since coming to Grace Church and so far it had served both him and the congregation well. His morning ritual was to stop at B&C (bagels and coffee) and then get lost in the hills surrounding Santa Fe. He tried to set a different pace each Friday; trail running one week, hiking the next, maybe mountain biking the next. The variety was good for his muscles. The different rhythms also caused him to see different things; what is good for the body is often good for the soul. Today's rhythm would be one of his favorites — the leisurely stroll.

There were occasional Fridays when the needs of the many outweighed the needs of the one: a church member having open-heart surgery, a funeral to officiate, a desperate call from someone in need. But besides a lunch invitation, this Friday was free and clear, and Jordan was grateful for that. With the expect-the-unexpected Soup Kitchen on tomorrow's schedule, it would be nice to greet Saturday with a fresh face.

Jordan ran down his pack list but was convinced he was forgetting something. He had been distracted ever since he woke up; the last thing on his mind the night before was the first thing on it this morning. He could not shake Tutu's words about Stanford student Amy Biehl: *Ironically, she was stabbed to death by four young antiapartheid fighters, who saw only the color of her skin.* Jordan rubbed his ebony arms.

He smiled, remembering two statements made the first day he preached at Grace Church — one from a man, one from a child. The man shook his hand, introduced himself, and said, "I'm color-blind. I don't see color; I just see people." Jordan had heard the sentiment or variations of it many times; it sounded so very spiritual, but it never failed to cause a knot in his stomach. A few moments later, the child, who he would come to know as Kate Dobbins, reached out and touched his hand: "Your black skin is so pretty."

The word "black" jogged his memory; he had forgotten to pack his Moleskine journal. He liked to keep it with him on Friday mornings to record things he saw or felt. He grabbed it and a pen from the kitchen table, dated the next blank page, and wrote: *I am not only the color of my skin, but I am a black man.*

The bagel shop was just a few minutes from Jordan's apartment, enough time for NPR to tell a story:

Ten years ago, a huge windstorm struck the remote Boundary Waters Canoe Area Wilderness in northern Minnesota. In just thirty minutes, winds of up to ninety miles per hour toppled 35 million trees in an area of more than 500 square miles. Campers were trapped ... it took three weeks to get everyone out. Now, the forest is growing back, and in spite of the way it has changed, people are still flocking to the Boundary Waters ...

Today, the big trees that have been lying there for ten years break when they are stepped on. University of Minnesota ecologist Lee Frelich says there will be fewer pines; the forest has jumped ahead to the next generation of trees: spruce, cedar, and fir.

"In this case, the wind came and wiped out the old pine forest in a few minutes, and they were able to start taking over immediately because they were small seedlings on the forest floor," Frelich says. And he says they're growing like mad. "While it was sad to see the big old pines go down, it's a good reminder that in nature, the only constant is change."

Jordan put the car in park, turned off the engine, and noticed his was the only vehicle in front of the shop. A sign was taped to the shop door:

> Due to a death in the family, B&C will be closed
> until further notice. We apologize for the inconvenience
> and appreciate your thoughts.

"Alright, Lord. I'm listening. *The only constant is change,* right?" Jordan believed a form of prayer was paying attention; praying with your eyes open. He held that it was much more beneficial than the usual bow-your-head-close-your-eyes. He remembered another bagel shop over near the campus. It was a little out of the way, but being off course was what Friday was all about.

The other shop was open and busy — no doubt benefitting from B&C's unfortunate status — so busy, in fact, that Jordan had to park beside a dumpster essentially behind the shop. As he walked in, he saw a few businessmen in Friday casual; two jogger moms with toddlers in tow; and a table of men, Bibles spread in front of them, loudly talking prophecy. He noticed a familiar face or two at the gathering of men.

It was Friday but Jordan didn't believe in removing the pastor hat on his day off. He had found over the years that noticing and greeting people is a small act but possibly one of the most significant things he could do. He did not believe in a clergy/laity divide, but he also knew that most people viewed ministers as God's representatives. It's just the way it is. If Jordan stopped and took notice of them, maybe that meant God did too. But it was a tension; the numerous minister scandals of recent years had just about worn away any public trust in men of the cloth. Still, he was a pastor, even on Fridays.

Jordan stepped toward the table of familiar faces to give a pastoral greeting; it was all of two steps in the cramped shop. He looked but didn't see anything on the table but Bibles and notepads. The group's obvious alpha male followed Jordan's eyes: "Man does not live by bread, right Pastor?"

"As I recall," Jordan said, "the verse says 'Man does not live by bread *alone*.' One of those pastries on the counter might bring a whole new depth to your study."

Several of the men laughed, but not alpha male. He made direct eye contact with Jordan. "We're feasting on the Word.

Right now we're discussing 2 Timothy 3: '… in the last days … men will be lovers of pleasure rather than lovers of God … they will not endure sound doctrine; but wanting to have their ears tickled, they will accumulate for themselves teachers in accordance with their own desires.' I'm sure you know the verses." All eyes at the table, as well as in the shop, were on Jordan for his reaction; he could feel them. Jordan sighed and smiled. He knew a theological scrapper when he heard one; this was not a moment to try to make an impact, but rather leave just a hint of Jesus. He remembered a friend's blog post he'd read a couple of days ago:

> Lately, there seem to be a lot of people wanting to make an *impact* on this world for Jesus. Leadership gurus want to *impact* the church. Student leaders are mobilizing to *impact* the next generation. I've even heard certain artists who are writing or singing or something to *impact* the culture.
>
> But I believe words mean things. So I looked up this six-letter arrangement to clarify the definition: to collide forcibly with; to strike. I then checked some related words: *concussion, hammering, onslaught, ramming, sideswipe, tremor, wallop,* and who could resist *whomp*. Now, in the interest of fairness, there are related words that ring all nice and smart like *etch* or *imprint,* but they don't stand much of a chance next to *mauling.*
>
> I don't believe Jesus wants us to do this. I really don't.
>
> Do you know the words *trace* or *whiff* or *hint* or *brush*? For example—"Jimmy slumped in right field, one cleat on top of

the other, close to the fence. Not a single ball came his direction all evening. But the fence was lined with honeysuckle, the whiff of which reminded him of the girl who now sat in front of him in science class. Jimmy liked playing right field."

I believe that's what Jesus wants us to do. Leave hints or traces or whiffs of grace and mercy and forgiveness, words that mean something, in the lives of those both near and far.

But you say, what about the incident when Jesus wove a rope and got busy turning over the tables of the money changers? That was quite impactful, wasn't it? Yes, I know; it's in there, so it counts. But I wonder sometimes if after the *onslaught*, Jesus sighed and chuckled to himself, "I'm not so sure what good that did." And maybe that chuckle came to mind when Peter drew his sword in the garden and whomped off that soldier's ear and Jesus said, "Peter, not this way" and then he put that ear right back where it came from, just like that … a little hint of miracle before the mob made their *impact*.

●●●

"Men, I'm always encouraged when I see believers wrestling with Scripture, fighting the good fight. Just don't miss the forest, alright? I hope you all have a good day."

Jordan stepped away and heard the alpha male jump right back in where he left off earlier. The middle-aged man at the counter rolled his eyes and smiled as Jordan approached. He was sporting a handlebar mustache and a *Live Strong* bracelet. "What can I do for you this morning?"

"I'd like a tall house blend with room for cream and two asiago cheese bagels, heavy on the cream cheese — everything to go."

"My pleasure. Will that be all?"

Jordan didn't miss a beat, but lowered his voice. "And I'd like a cherry danish delivered to each of the men around that table. But not until I'm out the door — deal?"

The man smiled again. "A subversive Samaritan. Nice, very nice." The man's words hinted at some familiarity with Scripture. "Did I overhear you're a pastor?"

Jordan nodded. "Grace Church here in town. Say, are the danishes homemade?"

"My wife and I make them fresh every day. Why do you ask?"

"Our church offers hot soup twice a month and tomorrow is our next offering … any chance I could order some and pick them up in the morning? I'd need about three dozen."

"It's a little late notice … are you only expecting thirty-six people?"

"No, I'm expecting about a hundred. But if I broke them and blessed them, there might even be leftovers." A second scriptural allusion was a stretch, but Jordan was willing to roll the pastoral dice. He extended his hand. "I'm Jordan. I could be here as soon as you open up."

The man seemed to think a minute, wiped his hands on his apron, and then reached across the counter to meet Jordan's hand. "Fish and loaves and danishes; sounds like you serve up quite a meal. I'm Rex. I don't live far from Grace. I could drop them off on my way in; it'd be about 5:30. Five dozen, right?"

Jordan paused. "Uh, yes, that's what I said."

Rex pushed a business card across the counter. "My cell number's at the bottom if something changes. See you bright and early, as they say."

Jordan checked his bag as he left the shop. He didn't doubt people, but he still liked to make sure he got what he ordered. Coffee, two bagels ... and a cherry danish. "Nice, very nice." As Jordan walked out to his car, he couldn't help but notice the figure on the bench across the street. He wasn't sure at first, but then the jacket gave him away. Louis.

A good friend from seminary had given Jordan the jacket one Christmas. They had taken a trip to experience autumn in New York and were not disappointed. A highlight of the week was getting tickets for Letterman. Jordan had been chosen from the audience to play "Know Your Current Events" — and he was the only person who answered all of the questions correctly. Letterman joked that knowing God so well might be an unfair advantage. The baseball jacket was green with yellow sleeves with the *Late Night* logo across the back. As far as Jordan knew, there was only one like it in Santa Fe, possibly even all of New Mexico.

He wore it one Saturday to the Soup Kitchen, the same day Louis showed up for the first time. He briefly welcomed the older man, got his name, and then left him alone. He could sense Louis was skittish. He could also tell the man liked his jacket. As the meal came to a close, Jordan had a gut feeling and followed it. He approached the newcomer, took off his jacket, and draped it over the chair beside Louis. "It'll keep you warm. I'd like for you to have it." Every other Saturday since then, Louis showed up for a hot bowl. Regardless of the weather, Louis wore the jacket. His moves were still full of caution, but he would always acknowledge Jordan; he called him "Preacher."

Jordan crossed the street and stood a few steps back from the bench, facing the man's back. "Louis?" For a moment, he couldn't tell if the jacket wrapped someone dead or alive. Louis began to slowly roll over but cringed halfway; only his head completed the turn. "Louis, it's Pastor Ross. Are you alright?"

The man's eyes focused through caked on sleep. "P … P … Preacher?"

"Can I help you sit up?" Jordan didn't rush in, but he didn't wait for Louis to answer either. He sat his breakfast bag beside the bench and extended his arm to Louis, much like a groomsman would offer a bridesmaid. Louis slowly curled up and hooked his arm in Jordan's. "Gonna have to pull, Preacher."

The next couple of seconds were more Jordan than Louis, but the man was finally in a slouched-upright position and offered a question: "Jesus H. tell you it was me?"

"No … D. Letterman. You look hurt, Louis."

"Been broke before. You go now."

Jordan hesitated, weighed the moment, and then reached into his breakfast bag. "Alright. I'll see you tomorrow at lunch — don't forget. These are on the menu." Jordan placed the cherry danish on a napkin beside Louis. "Coffee too — want it?"

"Keep it. Go on."

As the young pastor drove away, Louis nibbled his danish while a table of men in the coffee shop only steps away temporarily ceased all talk of *last days* and took their first bites.

●●●

Sam had a class at ten o'clock and an appointment with a student at 11:15, after which she could turn her attention to Friday night's dinner. Phillip had taken the girls to school so she had a few minutes to call Luci and invite them over. She sat down on the bed and as she grabbed her cell, it started ringing. The small screen displayed a familiar name and face, but Sam and her brother usually talked on Sunday nights.

"Ben, what is it?"

"Dad's in the hospital. He fell in the bathroom, hit his face against the sink. Nothing's broken, but he's got a shiner and two less teeth. The nurse said he was dehydrated too. They want to watch him, administer some fluids, and possibly run a few tests."

"Ben, he could have broken a hip or something."

"Yes, Sam, he could have, but he didn't. Listen, I think he's okay; I just wanted you to know. He did too."

"Can I talk to him?"

"He's asleep right now. They gave him something for the pain and it knocked him out. I'm in the cafeteria getting something to eat."

"Ben, I want to talk to him when he's awake, alright?"

"I promise, Sam. But don't you have classes this morning?"

"That doesn't matter. I want to talk to him when he's awake. Ben, thank you for being there."

"I'll call you. You're welcome."

There were times when the South Pole felt closer than Kansas. This was one of those times. Sam picked up the frame on the nightstand; a picture of the girls surrounding her dad. Her finger traced his outline as a tear fell. "Jesus, I feel so far away."

"Sam?" Phillip's voice was followed by the back door closing.

"I'm in the bedroom, Phillip."

Phillip focused on his hands and the hot cup he was carrying. "I brought you a chai. The girls were ... Sam, what's wrong?"

"It's Dad. He fell. Nothing's broken, but they're going to run some tests."

"Do you think we need to go? I can rearrange things."

"No, not today. Ben is there with him. Besides, you've got your meeting at noon and I feel like dinner tonight with Luci and her boys is important."

"So you've called and they can come?"

"No, Ben called just as I was getting ready to dial the number. But I really believe they'll be able to come. I do. You'll pick up the girls and I'll meet you here at three?"

"Okay. Sam, I'm sorry Dad fell and we're not there. When I first came in the room, I thought you were going to tell me that Dad died; that's a call I'm not quite ready for. I'm thankful Ben's there."

Sam stood and stepped into Phillip's embrace. "Me too."

●●●

As she rifled through her bag looking for the pack of peanut-butter crackers, Luci felt the phone vibrate. She didn't recognize the number.

"Hello, this is Luci."

"Luci, this is Samantha Dobbins, from last night."

"Oh,... hello." She was a little surprised. "Thanks so much for stopping to help me. My father is checking on the truck today."

"I'm glad he's there to help you, Luci." Sam paused as she gathered her courage. "Have I caught you at a bad time?"

"No, it's alright. I'm on a break for a few."

"Luci, I'm calling because, well, I know this sounds strange, but my husband and I would like to invite you and your boys over for dinner tonight."

There was silence on the phone. It was probably only a couple of seconds, but Sam was sure it was five minutes.

"That's kind of you, but why? We're really not a pity case."

Sam knew it was a fair question; in fact, it was a good question. What was it about this lady and her broken-down pickup and her fallen soldier of a husband and her two fatherless sons? There was so much it could be about, but maybe, for now at least, it was that something had worked itself into her heart and that something was a name: *Luci*. And she could not forget it.

"I'm not entirely sure, Luci ... no strings attached, alright? A meal and the chance to get to know you a little better. It's not pity. Please say you'll come."

Luci was feeling a mix of emotions all at once. She hated pity and wanted no part of it; but that's not what she heard in Sam's voice. She had stopped last night as Sam drove away and thought, *It would be so nice to have a friend like her.* The prospect of someone not wanting anything but to enjoy her presence was like something from a dream. But what she didn't need was a guilt-ridden, temporary friend who would disappear once the Good Samaritan novelty wore off. Too much had been taken already.

With a small hesitation in her voice, she said, "What time were you thinking? We really couldn't be anywhere before six o'clock."

"Six o'clock is perfect, Luci. But what about your truck—do I need to come get you?"

"No, my father can drop us by; it'll give him something to do and he likes doing things."

"Luci, is there anything your boys won't eat?"

"Not on this planet. I'm sorry but I've got to get back to work."

"Sure. Thanks for your time. We'll see you at six then."

Luci wrote down the address and said good-bye. She still had a moment before returning to the hospital floor. She dialed her father's number. "Dad? I just wanted to check on the truck."

"I'm looking it over now. Is everything okay there?"

Luci thought a second before she answered. "Maybe."

●◗●

Jordan pulled into the parking lot at St. John's College and prepared to start one of the most popular hiking trails in

Santa Fe—the Atalaya Mountain Trail. Today's rhythm was to be leisurely, so he felt a seven-mile loop to be about perfect, although his stroll would turn into an honest-to-goodness hike as he neared the peak. His efforts would be rewarded with views from the top of 9,121-foot Atalaya Mountain; the perspective on the Rio Grande valley below was simply breathtaking.

Jordan laced his boots, shouldered his Osprey daypack, and began the day's stroll. He loved Santa Fe's emphasis on the care of creation. It took many forms, such as the city council's recent unanimous approval of a Green Building Code for new residential construction. This was a major step in the city's commitment to the U.S. Mayors' Climate Protection Agreement. Local groups were organized and strong, able to affect policy and people.

Jordan had always held deep affection for the natural world. His mother was forever showing him things, pointing out the grandeur of God in cosmopolitan Boston: the honey locust trees and ginkgos that lined sidewalks; the ruby-throated hummingbirds; the New England wildflowers like sea lavender and meadow sage. But a seminary professor had introduced him to the writings of a certain Kentucky farmer/poet named Wendell Berry who built upon the foundation Jordan's mother had laid. Affection evolved into activism.

> The ecological teaching of the Bible is simply inescapable: God made the world because He wanted it made. He thinks the world is good, and He loves it. It is His world; He has never relinquished title to it. And He has never revoked

the conditions, bearing on His gift to us of the use of it, that oblige us to take excellent care of it. If God loves the world, then how might any person of faith be excused for not loving it or justified in destroying it?

—Wendell Berry, *What Are People For?*

Jordan believed the heavyweights in the evangelical movement had been slow to embrace this; however, things were changing. Younger voices of faith were interested in ecological salvation as well as personal salvation; *for God so loved the world* was a phrase both deep and wide.

Under Jordan's leadership, Grace Church now had a line item in the budget for creation care. The plan was to have two emphases every year: promoting education and a gradual change of lifestyle. The second Sunday of next month would be the first emphasis of this year. The morning's service would hold sermon and song focused on *our Father's world*, followed by a distribution of low-flow showerheads and faucet aerators to low-income and working families in the congregation. These two simple-to-install devices are the single most effective ways to conserve water in the home; they can reduce home water consumption by as much as 50 percent and reduce the energy cost of heating water by almost 50 percent as well.

But that was still several weeks away. Today Jordan's thoughts were still on the Good Samaritan; Sunday was a comin'.

"A man was going down from Jerusalem to Jericho, when he fell into the hands of robbers. They stripped him of his clothes, beat him and went away, leaving him half dead. A priest happened to be going down the same road, and when he saw the man, he passed by on the other side. So too, a Levite, when he came to the place and saw him, passed by on the other side."

—Luke 10:30–32

Now that he was some distance from the coffee shop experience and down the trail, he felt free to voice his lament to God. His father had taught him to take it *all* to God in prayer, even his anger: "Jordan, don't believe for one minute that God can't handle your rant. He's God."

Jordan had read where the writer Anna Quindlen said her greatest shortcoming as a writer was that she had an extremely happy childhood. There were traces of that statement that Jordan believed to be true about himself; he had been blessed with good parents.

Jordan began an animated muttering to himself. "Alright, Lord, I believe you can handle this, so here goes. From the sleep in his eyes and his difficulty turning over, it was obvious that Louis had been on that park bench most, if not all, of last night. All the parking spaces at Rex's shop face that bench and every one of them was taken when I drove up, so every one of those Bible studying men had to have seen Louis. But they passed by. And for what? To study your words and endure sound doctrine? In an effort to keep their ears from being tickled they closed their eyes …" Jordan calmed down momentarily as a trio of trail runners approached. Sweat-soaked shirts and a couple of bloody knees revealed their commitment. Once they passed, Jordan continued. " ... they closed their eyes to ... yeah, right, in the last days men will be lovers of pleasure, the pleasure of avoiding the other side." The first leg of the trail was relatively flat but Jordan's heart rate was already up; he realized he was rushing his stroll.

He slowed down. Several in the church had urged him to read Malcolm Gladwell's *The Tipping Point*. He did. He appreciated the stories, especially the experiment using the group of seminarians at Princeton representing a cross section of different religious and moral orientations. Each student was asked to prepare a talk on a biblical theme and was then informed it was to be presented in another building. As the student traveled to the next building, each one encountered a "victim" slumped in a doorway (coughing, groaning). The question was *Who would stop and help?*

Half of the students were assigned the parable of the Good Samaritan; the others were assigned a different topic. Some of the students were told they were late and should hurry; some were told they had just enough time to get to the recording room; and finally some were told they would arrive early.

The results were a nod to the power of circumstance. To the question of *Who would stop and help?* the answer was, *Those who weren't in a hurry.* Religious background, moral orientation, and even being assigned the parable of the Good Samaritan didn't make a difference.

Tipping points to the side, Jordan wasn't quite ready to concede that the Bible study men that morning were simply in a hurry. If that was true, then the question was, *What were they hurrying to?* Answer — *inside.* The men were rushing inside the coffee shop, inside their group, inside the book. Thoreau called the Bible a hypaethral book, best read "open to the sky." Jordan couldn't see how God's hypaethral book could lead you to an inside, roofed-over faith.

As he reached the peak of Atalaya Mountain, blood was flooding Jordan's quads and he felt like he was breathing through a straw; he loved it. He found a welcoming ponderosa pine and decided to sit awhile. The sky before him was a blue never found in Crayola boxes. After some water and M&Ms, Jordan pulled his Bible from the pack. He found his sermon passage and prayed, "Speak, Lord, for your servant is listening."

"A priest happened to be going down the same road, and when he saw the man, he passed by on the other side. So too, a Levite, when he came to the place and saw him, passed by on the other side."

The first thing that came to Jordan's mind were lines from a Wendell Berry poem:

Do not think me gentle
because I speak in praise of gentleness …
I am a man crude as any …

He laughed to himself. It seemed so much easier to hear God at 9,121 feet. "Okay, Lord, anger endures for the trail, but clarity comes at the peak, right? Yes, I am a man as crude and unseeing as those men this morning. I have rushed and hurried past more people than I care to think about, many times in the context of church or worship. *I* am the priest and the Levite. Alright, I'm still listening."

And maybe it was not only easier to hear but also to see at that altitude. Jordan began to see the faces of the men in the coffee shop, one by one, as well as the faces of Louis and Rex, even his own. "We're all the priest and the Levite, but we're also the man on the side of the road, aren't we? Whether from the actions of others, our own poor choices, or simply the presence of evil in our world, we're all beaten, bruised, robbed, and left half-dead. Why is it so hard for us to admit our need?"

●●●

"Phillip, I just left the conference center. I should arrive in Santa Fe within the hour; the directions to the restaurant are in my GPS."

"Sounds great, Kyle. I'll go ahead and get a table. My pastor may join us, okay? He's a good guy."

"Look forward to meeting him. I'll see you soon."

Barely thirty years old and newly engaged, Kyle Simpson would be leading the team to Kagoma next month. Phillip had talked with him several times on the phone, but Kyle's spur-of-the-moment trip to Glorieta placed him literally in Phillip's backyard. Phillip was excited to at last meet the young man he would be spending a fair amount time with in the weeks ahead. But he was also slightly concerned; in their recent phone conversations, Kyle had sounded agitated. Phillip couldn't put his finger on it, but something about Kyle reminded him of someone he used to know.

●●●

Jordan had agreed to meet Phillip for lunch, but now he almost regretted the decision. He was quite sure he could sit in the slight shade of the ponderosa pine and just *be* for the rest of the day. His sermon thoughts continued. "We're all the men on the sides of the road … maybe nothing starts until we can identify with them … if we can't see ourselves as those characters, it's still an us/them, outside/inside story."

"A Samaritan traveling the road came on him. When he saw the man's condition, his heart went out to him. He gave him first aid, disinfecting and bandaging his wounds. Then he lifted him onto his donkey, led him to an inn, and made him comfortable. In the morning he took out two silver coins and gave them to the innkeeper, saying, 'Take good care of him. If it costs any more, put it on my bill — I'll pay you on my way back.'"

— Luke 10:33 – 35, *The Message*

"And if we're all the men on the sides of the road, then what about the Good Samaritan? That's you, isn't it Lord?" Jordan usually kept his muttering to a mutter, but he realized he had just said that out loud and quite loud at that. He looked around, figuring on finding several pairs of eyes focused on him. But no one seemed to be paying any attention at all, as if a black man beneath a blue sky squatting against a pine tree at 9,000 feet talking to himself was something you see every day. He wondered if it would be different if he were bleeding profusely or moaning in agony. It might not.

Friday

There were a few things Jordan had learned in his years of ministry. One was that the mountaintop experiences are great, but you can't stay there; you have to go back down. And so he began his trek down the mountain. Clouds were building in the distance. Santa Fe might get an afternoon shower.

● ● ●

Sam's 11:15 appointment called at 11:16 and canceled. In a way, she was glad. There was so much on her mind right now, the student would have gotten half her focus and Sam always believed they deserved her full attention. She hoped Ben would call soon. At 11:20, he did.

"Sam, Da ... Dad's gone."

"What?! Where did he go? How did he leave the hospital? Weren't you there with him?"

"Sam, you're not hearing me. Dad just died. He went into cardiac arrest and they tried, longer than they probably should have ... but we lost him, Sam. Dad's gone."

"G ... give me a minute." And Ben did; a moment of silence held between a brother and his sister. "You were there with him, Ben? He wasn't alone?"

"I was there, Sam. I was with Dad."

"Oh, Ben. I ... I'm not ready for this."

"Me neither, Sam."

"Ben, I need to call Phillip."

"Yes, call Phillip, figure out when you're coming, and then call me back in a little while. There's no need for us to scramble around; Dad had everything in order, his decisions have all been made. It would grieve him to see us rushing all around. You know what he always said, Sam."

"Yes — 'rushing folks miss things.' How many times did I hear him say that?"

"Enough that we'd remember it. I cannot remember the man ever running a yellow light. You do know how much he loved you, right?"

"He loved us both, Ben."

"He was a good man, Sam. A good man."

"I can't thank you enough for being there, Ben. I'll call you back. Oh, Lord … I'm going to miss him."

"Me too."

Of all the things to think about in a moment like this, Sam remembered a story she'd heard about a group of hikers who descended into the Grand Canyon on September 10, 2001 and came out two days later. They'd had no access to news or contact with other hikers. They emerged to a completely different world, one that no longer held the Towers and was now wrapped in shades of fear. Sam felt that way after Ben's call. She now lived in a changed world. It was not a tower that fell, but the tallest tree in her forest, one of the old growth pines … her dad.

●●●

Isabel had seen the man cursing at the car as it drove by. He hobbled back and collapsed on his bench; the way he walked indicated he might be hurt. She felt drawn to him; she sensed no threat. As she approached, it was obvious he was living in the shadows of Santa Fe; Isabel felt that way many days too. Based on that common ground, she spoke and sat and offered him what she had — a drag on her cigarette. He didn't speak but accepted the smoke. He finally said something to the effect of "they'll kill ya" and she agreed.

He began to dig in the pockets of his jacket. She tensed a little as she could sense he was becoming agitated. But then the tension left. He reached over to hand her something, but there was nothing in his hand. He pressed the hand closer to her: "Take it." Isabel accepted whatever it was he was giving in return. "Fair?" She nodded and offered another drag.

There was no reason to linger. He started to hand back the cigarette when Isabel said, "Keep it." The man started to rummage again in his pockets but she stopped him by putting her hand on the arm of his jacket. "Really … just keep it." She stood and walked away.

She had never known her father. Her earliest memories were of a mother only and those had almost faded away. As she looked back at the man on the bench, she wondered if he was a father and if he was, where were his children? Did they not remember him at all, like Isabel? Or did they remember him and look for him every day to return, waiting at some picture window like in the movies? Then again, what if he chose to leave, deciding to not see his children again? Isabel wondered if that was how it was with her father; he saw who was in the room, Isabel and her mother, and the two of them were either too much or not enough, and he made the decision to walk away.

She wondered if she had any of her father's traits — eye color, personality, skin tone. There was no way to know. Isabel was not even sure which traits might have been inherited from her mother. Her still-vivid, final memory of her was a crazy-eyed woman trying to eat pages from a Bible.

Once, when leaving a hotel through the shadows, Isabel overheard a man talking: "Everyone here is lonely. This is a very lonely city." She thought the man told the truth. The only consistent person in her life had been the woman. She was not Isabel's mother or even related at all by blood. But she had been there all along. Isabel knew the woman had rarely acted warmly toward her, like a mother might act toward her own. Sure, she repeatedly told Isabel, "You're mine," but the words usually felt cold and hard. And lonely.

All sorrows are less with bread.

Miguel de Cervantes,
Don Quixote

Sam knew her dad's death would hit Phillip hard. He had not been *like* a father to Phillip; he *had* been a father. "Jesus, please have mercy on us today — on Ben, Phillip, the girls, me ... all of us. I'm not ready for this."

She walked out to the courtyard of St. John's to call Phillip. She stopped and sat in front of the small garden pond filled with koi. This place was usually a busy thoroughfare on campus, but by 11:30 on a Friday morning almost everyone had already begun the weekend. Her father had visited the campus a few times. He thought the koi were absolutely lovely and would sit and watch them in fascination while students passed by without as much as a glance. Sam could hear his voice: "God hands man a common carp and with a little attention to breeding, this is the colorful result. Lovely, like angels. Still, everyone passes them by. What does an angel have to do to get noticed around here?"

Her tears fell from the memory as she dialed Phillip's number.

"Hi. I thought you had an appointment?"

"She canceled. Phillip, I just … talked to B …" Her voice broke.

"To Ben? Sam, is Dad alright?"

"No. Dad died a few minutes ago. He's gone, Phillip."

The koi would swim for a moment in the deep shadows and then rise, gracing the surface with their bright orange and white. The Dobbins' phone conversation took on the same rhythm — silence and tears followed by vivid words of affection.

"I'll be right there. Where are you?"

"I'm sitting outside at school. But I want you to keep your lunch appointment with Kyle. It's important, really, I want you to. Call me when you're finished and we can go together to tell the girls." One of the older koi surfaced, a faded white similar to the color of a certain old pickup. "Oh, Phillip, I had already invited Luci to dinner tonight and she accepted …"

"Sam, you told me you felt dinner tonight with Luci and her boys was important — remember? I'm feeling the same thing, I don't know why, but I do. Sam?"

"I'm here, Phillip. And the feeling about Luci is still as strong, even after hearing about Dad. Do you think we're inviting them into something awkward though? Let's just try to put ourselves in her shoes."

Phillip waited a moment before responding. "Now we *are* in her shoes. She lost a man she loved. We've lost a man we loved …" Phillip didn't have to finish his sentence; Sam understood and agreed. "Besides, we both know what Dad would say."

Fresh tears filled Sam's eyes. A bright orange koi broke the surface, then a smile broke on Sam's face. "He'd say, 'Women and children first.'"

●●●

Elly finished her two-hour shift in the school bookstore. As she left the student center, she immediately noticed Dr. Dobbins sitting on the other side of the commons, by the small garden pool; she looked to be crying. Elly quickly crossed over.

"Dr. Dobbins? Is something wrong?"

"Hi, Elly." Sam kept staring straight ahead but patted the empty space beside her on the bench; Elly accepted the invitation. "I just got news that my dad died, Elly."

"Oh, Dr. Dobbins. Bless your heart."

Sam turned and looked directly into Elly's eyes; she knew the power of words, after all, she lived with a poet. There are times, maybe slivers of time, when the right word or phrase is like the biblical description: *apples of gold in settings of silver.* In that moment, Elly's "bless your heart" was just such an offering. Sam had heard that phrase in the Kansas of her youth at least a million times, maybe more. Many times the words rang hollow, a thoughtless expression people parroted when they didn't know anything else to say. But sometimes the three words rang bell-struck true — another human being taking the time to cross to the other side and ask/hope/pray a blessing into the heart of another, that deep place we all hold in common. The wise men brought three gifts of verifiable worth that blessed night; Elly the wise college girl brought three words of inestimable value that grief-heavy day.

"Alright, I know you can use my help today then. Let me take care of a couple of errands and I'll be right over." Elly was already mentally rearranging her preset plans.

"Thank you, Elly. I hadn't told you yet, but in addition to you, we had invited a young mother and her two sons over for dinner tonight. We've decided to stay tonight and have everyone over, then leave first thing tomorrow. So, yes, I'd love your help. Phillip's got a lunch appointment and then we're going to pick up the girls. Let me call you then."

Elly reached, took Sam's hand, and gently squeezed it before departing. For just a moment, a sun-faded bench by a pond filled with koi became the mourner's bench, not so much a place to repent of one's sin, as to share the weight of what it means to be human, to help bear another's burden.

●●●

Phillip and Jordan arrived at the restaurant a few minutes early. Phillip was glad as it gave him an opportunity to tell his pastor of the morning's news.

"Phillip, I am so sorry. Maybe we can reschedule the lunch for another time."

"No, I'm still going to meet Kyle and I would like you to be here. Sam and I have talked and we've decided to stay and see two things through today; we'll leave first thing in the morning. I know it sounds strange, but it feels right."

"If that's what you and Sam have decided, then it's not strange at all, Phillip. He was like a father to you, wasn't he?"

"Yes, he really was … a father …" Phillip had trouble finishing the thought. It was even more difficult to believe he was gone.

"I'd like to give Sam a quick call — do you think she's answering her cell?" Jordan stood and looked for a quiet corner.

"Thank you. Yes, I think she'll answer." Phillip watched as his pastor walked a few feet away and dialed the number. He was grateful for Jordan's presence.

A minute or two later a clean-cut young man wearing a T-shirt and those industrial-style khakis entered the room. Phillip guessed him to be Kyle Simpson.

Phillip stood to greet him. "Kyle?"

"Hi, Phillip." The young man extended his hand as he looked around. "Wasn't your pastor joining us?"

"Yes. Kyle Simpson, I'd like you to meet my pastor, Jordan Ross." Phillip welcomed Jordan back to the table. He then told Kyle what had happened in his family; he felt the young man deserved to know.

"I'm very sorry," Kyle said. "Sounds like you two were really close."

"We were."

Silence fell over the table for a moment, but then the waiter arrived and time began moving at its usual pace, the men ordering lunch plates and talking of the work Kyle was doing. Throughout it all, Phillip still sensed anger in the young man's voice. The next words from Kyle's mouth confirmed this.

"You know, I grew up believing that hate was the opposite of love, but it's not; the opposite is indifference. I've been over there enough times to see this; you'll see it too, Phillip. It drives you crazy. I've been writing letters all month to our donors demanding help, but people just don't get it."

Jordan sensed it as well and skillfully bent the direction of the conversation, asking Kyle about some of the people he was trying to help, maybe some personal stories. As Kyle followed Jordan's lead, Phillip realized who Kyle reminded him of—himself. He felt like he was sitting across from an earlier version of Phillip Dobbins: a young man who believed his way was the only and true way; someone who believed he was an emissary of God, when he was really an emissary of himself; a spirited defender with a position of righteousness and whose food was anger.

Phillip had once been a young, enthusiastic Good Samaritan, working with the Red Cross in Mexico, his valor and ethics less endearing to the people around him than he believed. He had railed against the details that donors seemed so interested in—*couldn't they get it?* His plans had been as grandiose as his ambition. Phillip did not believe this in itself a bad thing, but it does add to the burden of those around you.

And then one day, it was hard for Phillip to remember just why, he realized he no longer had any desire to be singled out for praise or even recognized as a smart man; all he needed to do was try to reduce the suffering where and when he found it. Phillip started doing what he could and then moving on. It was not long after that awakening that he met Sam. Sitting across from Kyle, he could see now that until that realization, it was quite impossible for a woman or anyone for that matter to love him. There was simply no room.

It would take time, but he hoped a similar realization would dawn on this young, feisty man he liked so much; a conversion of entering the misery around him instead of trying to beat it into submission. Yes, Phillip thought, time and perhaps the presence of an older man. But mixed with these feelings were traces of envy — he hoped Kyle would not lose his passion as the years and experiences took their inevitable toll. There was something to be said for the fire in the belly of this young man, what one poet referred to as a *difficult brilliance.* Sometimes Phillip wondered if he couldn't use a little rekindling in his own belly.

Phillip and Jordan waved good-bye as Kyle disappeared into the parking garage down the block. Jordan broke the moment's spell: "I'm glad you're in his life, Phillip."

"Why do you say that?" Phillip was interested in his pastor's take on Kyle.

"He is content to see but not meet the world. But give him time … I really like him; he reminds me of someone." Jordan smiled. "You'd better get home. Sam needs you. Let me get cleaned up and I'll be by to check on you all. I will be praying for you all this day, my friend."

Phillip believed *I'll be praying for you* usually meant little if anything — a phrase quickly spoken and ever more quickly forgotten. But standing beside his friend that day, it meant the world.

●●●

Once everyone was back home, Phillip held his daughters as he told them of their grandfather's death. Sarah and Lily were old enough to realize what had happened, but still young enough to quickly return to dolls and cartoons. Maggie showed her thirteen-year-old maturity by saying, "Now he's with Grammy." But it was Kate that Phillip worried about. With an older sister and younger twins, she was essentially in the middle, always feeling the press of things from both sides. She could have said something grown-up like Maggie, but she didn't. And she could have returned to play like the twins, but that didn't fit either. Phillip could see she didn't quite know what to do with herself.

Elly had arrived and made her way to each of the girls to express her sympathies. Then she stepped into action helping Sam prepare things for dinner. Maggie asked if she could help and was given several assignments. The twins were in the backyard, swinging. Kate and Phillip sat on the couch, momentarily without task or distraction. At last Phillip stood up: "Your mom said I could make polenta tonight; I need a few things from the store — wanna go?" He extended his hand to his middle daughter and she took it, holding on tight. Sam asked if they could remember two bags of ice as well; they said they could.

As Phillip turned his head to back the car, Kate broke the silence: "Daddy, the lady who's coming tonight — her husband died?"

"Yes, K. He was a soldier." Phillip waited for follow-up, but found none. He put the car in drive and headed down the street. "K., why did you want to know?"

"When we're all sitting around the table tonight, like we used to do at Pop's house ... I might go to pieces."

Phillip marveled at the little girl with his same last name, and especially at her choice of words. It wasn't more than two weeks ago that he'd been rereading a favorite novel, *The Maytrees* by Annie Dillard, and these words that were suddenly so appropriate:

> "If you were a prehistoric Aleut and your wife or husband died, your people braced your joints for grief. That is, they lashed hide bindings around your knees, ankles, elbows, shoulders, and hips. You could still move, barely, as if swaddled. Otherwise, the Aleuts said, in your grief you would go to pieces just as the skeleton would go to pieces. You would fall apart."

He eased the car over and reached across to the other side. As if to brace his daughter's joints for the grief that was there on that day and the grief that life would surely hold, he gently wrapped his hide around her shoulders. "If you do, K., I bet she'll understand."

"That's why I asked, Daddy."

●●●

Luci usually worked a four-day week in the ER. The ten-hour shifts were exhausting, but it was worth it to have the weekends free with the boys; even more worth it just to have a job. She had traded for this Friday shift with a coworker several weeks ago so she could go out for her birthday. If she could only have known then what she knew now, she would never have agreed to switch. Her birthday had been a disaster as she fell to pieces outside the restaurant and today's shift had been nonstop from the time she walked in the door. Plus, she didn't know what to do with *him*. A group of men smelling of coffee had brought him to the ER early that morning: sixtysomething-year-old male, possible broken ribs, possible mental condition, apparently homeless, David Letterman jacket. His eyes showed fear, exhaustion. Try as she might, she could not get him to give her his name. And getting the X-ray took four tries and a sedative.

The ER doctor on call was a friend of Luci's — super friendly, but definitely the boss. He called Luci over, a few steps from the patient, and was crystal clear: "Before your shift is over, he's gone. Did you ever get an X-ray?"

"Finally. They're not broken, just bruised. The guy's in a world of pain."

"Okay then, give him some Aleve, offer the rib belt, get him a milkshake from the cafeteria, and we move on. I hate it as much as you do — but in cases like these, do what you can, then go on your way. By all means, Luci, do the best you can … but before your shift …"

"I know, I know. It just shouldn't be this way."

"I agree, Luci. But it's the way things are. These folks are just too poor to make the news or the hospital bed."

Much of the news coverage these days concerns what some have called "the noveau poor" — stories like a policeman facing foreclosure in the suburbs or an office assistant working the local strip club on the weekends to make ends meet. But what about the people who were already poor to begin with — *the old poor? People like Louis?* With so much emphasis on Main Street, people on the backstreets are largely forgotten. Low-wage jobs once available to the long-term poor are now the domain of the laid-off, downsized, squeezed-out middle class. How are the old poor coping?

One of the families down the street from Luci was coping in an increasingly common way: simply increase the number of paying people per square foot. The last few times she had driven by the house, it looked like that fairy tale about the woman who lived in a shoe — men, women, children, even pets.

Although it was not the only reason, the local news reports tied conditions like this to job losses. With no paychecks coming in, people fall behind on their rent and, because there can be as long as a six-year wait for federal housing subsidies, they often have no alternative but to move in with people they know and sometimes, people they don't.

Luci knew of one social worker at the hospital who was attempting to help an elderly couple who had taken in six unrelated subtenants because the couple could no longer afford the $600-a-month rent on their two-bedroom apartment. The couple was now facing eviction and the husband fell last weekend and broke a hip.

The outward face of this overcrowding is erratic sleep schedules or long bathroom waits, but remove the mask and there is often domestic violence hidden underneath. Luci had been startled awake several nights by screams and yells coming from all the people who lived in the shoe.

●●●

As Luci turned back around, her pent-up frustration popped: "Jesus!"

"You know Jesus H.?"

You could have heard a pin drop in the holding area. For the first time all day, the man's eyes softened, not entirely, but Luci saw an opening, maybe enough to possibly get a name. "Jesus? Yes, I know him. He calls me 'Luci.' What does he call you?"

"What does he say to Luci?"

Back then, Luci had been saved and baptized, prayed regularly, and felt like Jesus listened. But that was before Kurt's death. *Now*, she mainly felt abandoned. She had been to church a few times after the funeral, looking for something or someone. Whatever it was she wanted or needed then, she didn't find it at church. She used to wonder why, but she hadn't thought about that in a long time.

All she could think of were the doctor's words from a moment ago; they would have to suffice. She looked at her patient and spoke directly: "What does Jesus say to me? Well, he says, 'Do what you can, then go on your way.'"

"That's what Luci gonna do for Louis?"

Their piecemeal conversation gave Luci new resolve. "Yes, it is. I'm going to give you something for your pain, bring you a chocolate milkshake, and discharge you. That's how it's going to go."

The man turned slightly toward the wall. "Old Louis likes vanilla."

◦◦◦

Jim and Linda didn't make it to Grace Church to deliver the grocery bags until almost 4:30 that afternoon. They had dropped what they were doing when Phillip called to tell them about Sam's dad. They pressed: "What can we do, Phillip?"

"Just go by … it's your presence, just your being there. Trust me. She'll be so glad to see you."

What they were "doing" before Phillip's call was preparing for their trip to the grocery store for a few items needed for Saturday. It was one of the ways Pastor Ross said they could help the day before *the day*. Being a part of the Soup Kitchen would be a totally new experience for them, like driving around Santa Fe late at night and considering how to be a part of the story of the orphans.

Phillip was right. As Sam opened the door to greet them, the first words out of her mouth were, "Oh, I'm so glad to see you."

Jim and Linda wrapped their arms around their good friend named Sam.

●●●

Luci yelled down the hall: "Boys, we probably need to go."

She was sure the boys would be fine this evening; it was herself she was worried about. It had only been a day since Sam and Phillip helped raise her spirits, but the experience with Louis had drained her. She had pushed him outside the ER door in a wheelchair to no one waiting. "You're sure there's no one I can call?"

"Did what you could. Now move on, Luci."

As Louis shuffled to the building's edge, she noticed his shoes — boots, about two sizes too large, even for the man's big frame. Luci whispered to herself: "Walking in someone else's shoes too."

The image of Louis was dissolved by her mother's voice: "Honey, I held the boys off as long as I could, but I'm pretty sure they snuck a snack right before you got home."

"It's okay, Mom. Thanks for trying."

Luci's dad walked in and joined the conversation. "I do hope you all have a good time tonight. These people sound nice."

Luci nodded. Then she thought about the fact that "nice" as defined by her father did not necessarily match her own thoughts. His "nice" meant something he was familiar with, usually along the lines of white people, white food, white cars, that sort of thing. "Dad, I know I asked if you would drive us, but if you're okay, I'd like to take the car. That way we can leave when we're ready."

"Oh, sure, sure. I'll get you the keys."

● ● ●

Phillip had prepared his egg-and-Gruyère polenta. Elly had made a double serving of her macaroni and cheese. Sam prepared a roast and Maggie and Kate tossed the salad. Drink options would be lemonade and tea. Pastor Ross had been by earlier and said he would swing back later with a couple of pies, so dessert was covered. As Sam looked around at everything prepared with time to spare, this dinner felt like God's will or something. She sure hoped it was.

Sam had talked to Ben several times throughout the afternoon. He approved of her plan to host dinner and come Saturday morning: "Dad would say 'Women and children first' or something like that. Sam, I want you to be thinking of something. Dad helped a lot of people over the years, probably more than you or I know. Folks will want to know where to send gifts. His affairs were all in order, everything's paid for. I don't need the money and it appears you and the poet are doing alright. Let's decide on something that matters, okay?"

Sam assured him it had already crossed her mind. And it really had—a living legacy, not to try to keep her father alive, but to keep alive the things he believed in, like helping people who needed help. "Yes, Ben, something that matters."

The clock chimed as the doorbell rang. "Six o'clock — right on time; I'll get it." As she headed for the door, she had a strange feeling, much like the one she felt when she stopped to help Luci last night. There had been no way of knowing what she was stepping into; tonight had the same sensation — what was on the other side of that front door? Samantha Dobbins had no idea, but there was only one way to find out — cross to the other side, welcome the stranger. Prayer always helped.

"Jesus, I stayed, we stayed, because it felt like the right thing to do. We're leaving in the morning, so for tonight please help us to do what we can and then move on. Amen."

A deep breath and Sam opened the door to Luci and Kurt Jr. and David Dillard. "Oh, I'm so glad to see you. Please, please come in."

Luci brought a small arrangement of flowers as her contribution for the evening. "Luci, they're beautiful," said Sam. "What are ... are these jasmine?"

"Yes. I grow them at home."

The Dillards were introduced all around. The girls asked the boys a silly question, "Do you want to go jump on the trampoline?" There are questions without answers and then there are questions that need no answer; this one was answered by the rush of children's feet. Elly was the last to come into the den; she had checked on the roast one final time. As she moved through the house, a smell caught her senses, reminding her of home. "Alright, who has jasmi ...?" She stopped as she saw the guest; it wasn't an awkward silence as much as slight shock.

"Hi, I'm Luci Dillard."

Elly's smile grew wide. "Shucks."

Elly's favorite word was the key that sprung the lock of memory for both women: a tube of lipstick, the brush of skin, tears. Elly and Luci both looked like they'd seen an angel.

"That day … I think you handed me my lipstick." It was getting clearer for Luci.

"Sure did. You just needed an extra hand. I'm Elly."

"Hello, Elly. That was the nicest thing anybody had done for me in a long time. I wished I could have thanked you … so, 'thank you.'"

Elly extended her hand to shake Luci's, then chuckled. "Gosh, you hardly have a hand big enough to shake. C'mon, let's get a vase for those flowers. I was hoping I'd see you again sometime." Luci followed Elly into the kitchen. Sam and Phillip were momentarily left alone.

"Didn't see that one coming," Phillip said. "It's almost like this evening was supposed to happen."

Sam nodded a wordless yes. "How about you check on the kids? I need to tell Luci about today, so ladies only in the kitchen for a minute."

Phillip put his arms around his wife's shoulders and drew her close. "Kate believes she'll understand, Sam."

"You and Kate talked about this?"

"In the car, for just a moment. In her words, she was afraid she might 'go to pieces tonight' if we're all sitting around the table eating, like at Dad's."

"I might join her, Phillip."

"Well, if we do, we do. I'll be outside with the kids."

●●●

Sam spoke the words and for a few moments the three women just cried. Some people make distinctions between empathy and sympathy; in these moments, there were no such nuances. The air in Sam's kitchen was filled with the root of both words: *pathos* — grief.

There were no words exchanged in the kitchen for almost a minute. In that sixty seconds approximately 200 people died around the world: some at the end of their lives; some caught unawares in the middle; still others at the very beginning, so fresh from God; some paupers; some in the working class; and some kings. But in that minute even some kings realized they were temporary.

"I'm so very sorry," Luci said. "I'm not sure we should be here right now. Why didn't you call and tell me what happened?"

"I thought if I did you wouldn't come, and we really wanted you to be here." Sam kept talking, but in spurts of thought, as if a ball of thread were unrolling: "I'm sorry, Luci, maybe … maybe I wasn't really … maybe I wasn't really thinking about you but me and … and doing something to maintain some order … oh, I'm sorry, Luci." Her assurance about the evening from a moment ago suddenly unraveled; she felt like someone broken down on the side of the road.

Elly stepped into the gap. "Coffee, Luci?" She had already poured a demitasse cup for Sam and herself.

"Yes, thank you. But do you have a real mug?"

Elly got tickled at Luci's question, as did Sam, and their tickling broke into laughter. It spread to Luci as well. For a few moments, they couldn't stop. A neighbor peeking in the window would have seen three women unable to decide whether they wanted to laugh or cry and that would have been about right.

"We do what we can to keep it together. When I got the news Kurt died, I made salsa, jars and jars of salsa. He loved the stuff. I think I believed if I made enough that he might walk in the kitchen, grab some chips and a bowl, and everything would be … and he would say, 'Good sals, Luce.' But he never did."

Elly handed Luci a real mug. "How long has he been gone?"

"It'll be a year on Sunday." Luci blew and sipped the hot coffee.

Elly asked one more. "How long were you married, Luci?"

The sip of hot coffee kept Luci from an immediate response. Sam helped in the moment by answering for her new friend: "Not long enough."

The weight of the moment was lightened when Luci noticed her coffee mug: the resurrection mug. It had been a gift from Sam's brother, Ben; he'd found it in a kitschy curio shop in Taos. A rendering of the Easter tomb scene graced the empty mug, but once hot coffee was poured, the stone vanished and Jesus appeared with open arms, ascending. Once the hot coffee was gone, the stone returned and Jesus disappeared. Sam and Ben laughed and laughed about it on the phone after it first arrived; Phillip just rolled his eyes.

"Interesting mug choice." Luci turned the mug so Sam and Elly could see.

"You did ask for a *real* mug." Elly winked at the grieving women. She might not always know the right thing to say, but she believed it was always worth a try.

●●●

Jordan couldn't decide whether he would stay or not. Sam and Phillip invited him to, but he just wasn't sure. He had asked if they had everything for tonight and Sam indicated there was no dessert. He was very thankful for that statement because it gave him something tangible to offer. He always offered prayer; it was a part of what he did, who he was. And he sincerely believed it accomplished things beyond what this world knows. But to be able to do something and see immediate results made him feel so good, so needed.

He stopped by The Village restaurant en route. The older waitress directed his attention to the three pies left: two strawberry rhubarbs and a key lime. "What'll it be, son?"

Jordan had noticed her name tag when he came in — *Leigh*. "Leigh, I need to provide some comfort to some people who are sad. What do you suggest?"

"By sad, what do you mean? Did they lose someone?"

"Yes, a father." Jordan found a lump in his throat.

Leigh turned and boxed up the two strawberry rhubarb pies without a word.

Jordan felt he had to ask, "So you don't think it would be good to have one of both, so they could choose?"

"Nothing eases the taste of grief in your mouth like strawberry rhubarb pie." Tears formed in Leigh's eyes as she said those words. Jordan believed he was in the presence of a witness, one who had been there and felt that on her own skin.

He handed her the twenty-dollar bill and she returned his change. "Thank you for your kindness, Leigh."

"Thank you for using my name when you spoke. I will light a candle for your friends."

As Jordan got back into his car, the lump in his throat made its way north. Tears streamed down his cheeks. The 3 x 5 card paperclipped to the visor caught his eye: *Be kind, for everyone you meet is fighting a great battle.* "Lord ..." He stopped his audible prayer; it seemed unnecessary for a moment. He did not believe the bread and wine of communion became the literal body and blood of Christ. He also did not believe it was merely a symbol. Something happened between those two extremes, something in the middle, best described as *mystery.* The strawberry rhubarb pies in the seat next to him now occupied that same mysterious middle. Leigh's kindness had changed them, made them more than they were. Jordan finished his prayer: "Lord, help us taste and see. Amen."

●◦●

"I hope you boys are hungry." Elly placed macaroni and cheese on the boys' plates and Sam followed in the assembly line with a slice of roast.

"We're starving," Kurt Jr. said. "We haven't eaten since prob'ly five o'clock."

The doorbell rang and Phillip excused himself from the kitchen. When he opened the front door, he found his pastor holding two pies and wearing a smile. "Pastor, if you come in, you have to stay."

"That's the deal?"

"That's the deal. Take it or leave them."

"Deal. How's it going in there?" Jordan asked, motioning toward the back of the house.

"I believe we made the right decision to stay. What kind of pies?"

"Strawberry rhubarb, both of them. *Leigh* at The Village helped me decide."

"Smart lady." Phillip led the way to the kitchen and introduced Jordan to Luci and her boys and asked everyone to pause for a blessing. His first thought was to ask Jordan to pray; it just seemed logical. But a second thought trumped his first; he would open it to the group. "Does anyone want to bless the food?" Phillip caught Kate's eyes as she stood beside the mother who had taught her children to pray in all times.

"I do, Dad."

Kate bowed her head and the rest in the room followed like obedient dominos, everyone, that is, except her father. Phillip would stand at the ready in case she needed him, in case the pieces started falling.

"Dear Je … wait, we need to hold hands." The heads, like fallen dominoes in rewind, raised, everyone took a hand without question, and all bowed once more, even her father this time, bound to one another by that most accessible of hides — the hands. "Dear Jesus, we're sad tonight. But we're happy that Mrs. Dillard and Kurt Jr. and David came over … and Pastor Ross too. Amen."

And in the wake of a child's prayer, grace abounded even more than it had a second ago. Or maybe it was just that Kate's words, along with the smell of jasmine and the presence of strawberry rhubarb pies, helped everyone be more aware of the presence of something that had been there all along, someone who brought comfort to all under the Dobbins' roof that evening, a *dear Jesus* large enough to hold both the sad and the happy and understand.

The kids finished their meal almost before the adults had a chance to sit down. "Maggie, why don't you all go outside, maybe jump for awhile, then we'll call you and we can have dessert?"

Maggie knew when her mother's question was really a statement; tonight, it was fine. "Sure, Mom. No problem. Just call us when the pie is ready." The kids all ran outside.

Seconds later Luci's youngest, David, ran back inside with a big, expectant smile on his face. "What kind of pie?"

Phillip looked in Jordan's direction. "David, you'll have to ask Pastor Ross; he brought the pies."

David looked directly at Jordan; his seven-year-old words were clear as he turned to go back outside: "Never mind. I don't like pie."

●●●

Jordan remembered the story of a little three-year-old girl. It was nap time in her classroom. She had already placed her cot on the floor, but then picked it up to move to the other side of the room. Her teacher asked about the move. She pointed to the four-year-old black child on a nearby cot and explained she couldn't sleep next to *those people* — they're "stinky." The classroom teacher told her to return to her original spot and not to use "hurting words."

When the children later went out to play, the director of the school called the three-year-old's parents for a meeting about her words. When the parents arrived — the father white and the mother half-white, half-Asian — they were stunned at the story. Everyone was certain of their innocence in the situation; the father even blaming another child's father as the corrupting influence — "a real redneck." Jordan wondered what had motivated David's comments.

●●●

Luci was completely red-faced. "Pastor Ross, I apologize. I don't know where that came from. I don't allow that kind of attitude in our home."

"Thank you, Luci. It always catches me a little off guard when it comes from a child."

"Kurt had several men in his unit who were African-American; they were over at our house all the time. That's been over a year ago, but ..." Luci was still blushing.

Elly quickly jumped in. "I don't believe kids are just parroting what they see or hear at home."

"Go on, Elly," Sam prompted.

"The usual, unfortunate response to what David said is, 'Well, they're just children. They don't know any better.' But at its core, that's a belief that children are empty vessels, mimicking what they see and hear from others until they reach a point when more in-depth thinking and processing starts taking place. But there's what adults think about children and then there's what children are actually doing. I'm not doing this justice, but some of the research indicates that kids as young as three, four, and five are taking their ever-increasing knowledge of the world and forming thoughts, opinions, and choosing words based on that understanding."

"David might have known better but said it anyway?" Luci was still embarrassed at the whole thing.

"Shucks, no, Luci. I'm saying that to think David expressed that because he heard it or saw it in you just doesn't hold water anymore. At least not for me."

"So maybe I'm not the world's worst mom?"

"Maybe not," Elly laughed. Elly's good nature was once again a saving grace. The rest of the table, including Jordan, laughed as well. "Pastor Ross, please don't hear me making light; racism is insidious, but the origins are so difficult to pinpoint."

"Not at all, Elly. I appreciated hearing your thoughts."

Phillip finished chewing his roast. "Luci, where did you grow up?"

"Most of my public school years were in north Texas. After I went to college, my parents moved to Oklahoma, but only an hour or so from where I grew up. My father lost his job not long after Kurt died. He and Mom live with us now."

"Were there racial struggles where you grew up?" Sam asked.

"Yes, but the different race that lived around us was Hispanic, not African-American. A Hispanic family moved into an older home in our neighborhood when I was in junior high school. They had a daughter, Ana; she and I were friends. She would come to our house and we would play or do homework, but each time, after she left, my mother would spray down my room with Lysol. It was horribly embarrassing."

Jordan asked, "Luci, did you ever say anything to your parents?"

"My mother wouldn't talk about it. I asked my father once and he said, 'They're not clean; you're lucky I allow her in here at all.' I never asked about it again; I really liked Ana. Look, I'm sorry my son drove our conversation down this road."

"It's okay, Luci," Sam said. "How about you and I go get the coffee and pie?" Luci was thankful for Sam's segue into something else.

"Sure, glad to help."

Phillip, Elly, and Jordan remained at the table. So did residue of the previous topic. Elly's curiosity got the best of her; it was, after all, her first time to meet Jordan. She had heard about him from Sam and Phillip; they had even invited her to Grace Church, but the timing had never been right. "Pastor Ross, where are you from? And yes, I just ended that question with a preposition, but I don't care." Phillip and Jordan laughed.

"I'll tell you a little but then I'm sorry, I have to go. Tomorrow is our church's Soup Kitchen and I need to prepare a few things. Okay, let's see … where am I from? I'm not even sure you know some of this, Phillip. I grew up in Boston; my father was an attorney and my mother was a botanist; I have two younger brothers. My parents were a mixed-race couple. They seemed almost oblivious to the fact, but my brothers and I struggled; we mixed it up quite a bit, much to my parents' chagrin. We were tough and always threw the first punch, so to speak. It was the '70s; a lot was going on in the country. The racism we experienced felt like systemic injustice and probably it was … probably still is. I do believe in such a thing. But after awhile, my focus shifted; I tried to choose my battles more carefully. You might say I moved from 'change the structure' to 'change the spirit.' I believe in the power of changing hearts first and foremost. Many of my friends disagree with me; in fact, my two brothers still do. But that's what I felt called to; it led me to Union Seminary in New York. I still feel the same way."

"What would you point to as the origins or roots of racism?" Phillip asked.

Jordan thought a moment. "The root of the problem is not racism; that's the symptom. The root begins … at the beginning, when we realize that we are living in a fallen world, full of fallen people. And fallen people go to great lengths to avoid taking care of each other. There's obviously more to that story, but I have to excuse myself. We'll fill in the blanks another time. Deal?" Jordan stood and extended his hand to Phillip.

Phillip stood and took his hand. "Deal. That okay with you, Elly?"

Elly's eyebrows shot up. "Avoiding taking care of the dishes?"

Jordan was pleased. "Touché, Elly. I am the chief of sinners. I'll see myself out, Phillip. Traveling mercies as you leave tomorrow."

Jordan reached across the table and shook hands with Elly, then stuck his head in the kitchen to say good-bye to Sam and Luci. "Sam, I'll be thinking about you all on your way to Kansas. Thank you for a wonderful meal."

"I'm glad you came. Please take the jasmine for the Soup Kitchen tomorrow; we're leaving in the morning and somebody else needs to enjoy the smell."

"I'll do it, Sam. Thanks. And it was nice meeting you, Luci. I hope to see you again sometime."

Luci suddenly thought about the plates in her hands. "But what about your piece of pie, Pastor Ross? You're the one who brought them."

"Tell you what. See if you can get David to eat a slice. If he does, tell him I'm glad he enjoyed it. If he won't, don't tell me."

Luci smiled. "Deal."

Jordan knew many who believed racists were only white-hooded, backwoods characters in front of burning crosses. Unfortunately, he believed, this only reinforced racism. He had long thought that maybe a shift was needed — "racist" no longer as a noun, but an adjective.

Jordan knew good and well there are those who experience the reality of inequality on a daily basis. Those who do not are privileged; they have the privilege of obliviousness. They simply do not have to think about it. This privilege often carries with it a color-blind approach to racism — i.e., discrimination is a thing of the past. Whereas many view the color-blind approach as non-racist, just as many hold that it only perpetuates racial inequality. Color blindness works if everyone exists on a level playing field. Jordan knew Jesus' words: "The poor you will always have with you …" He also knew that to believe and behave otherwise indicates a privilege, one of oblivion.

●●●

Luci and her boys said "thank you so much" and made their way home. Elly had stayed until the kitchen was clean. The girls were already asleep. Sam and Phillip slid into bed, tired, but good tired. And then they collapsed into each other, as if their bones had dissolved, and cried themselves to sleep.

●●●

Earlier in the day, Isabel stopped by St. John's to visit her *angels*. She had not been given details for Friday night; she had been told, "Just be ready." Isabel had learned that kind of vague instruction could mean just about anything. As she approached the koi pond, she saw a woman sitting there. At first, she considered slinking back, but then the woman leaned forward, like she might leave; it appeared she was crying. As Isabel walked up to the pond, the woman leaned back against the bench. Isabel had already committed herself to sitting at the pond's edge; she was close enough so the woman could see her. So she went ahead, sitting almost diagonally across from the woman.

The koi huddled close together beneath Isabel's shadow. The woman spoke: "They seem to like you." The woman sniffed and wiped her eyes.

Isabel surprised herself by asking, "Why are you so sad?"

The woman's voice was kind: "My father died this morning."

"I am sorry," Isabel said.

"Thank you. He did not suffer." The woman stood back up this time, intent on leaving.

"Was he beautiful?" Isabel asked.

The woman paused. It seemed the strangest of questions. "Beautiful? My father?" She paused again. "Yes, he was. I'm glad you asked." And then she walked away.

Isabel was surprised. Death was always the thing off the table; never talked about, but always there. This woman spoke of it freely, as if it were not an enemy. Isabel began talking in her mind's language to the koi beneath her feet:

If I had the chance, I would live my life differently. People who say they wouldn't change a thing are liars or fools. I have learned many things, so of course I would live it differently.

I would never do anything just for money, because every time I have, I have failed myself. I would learn to sing, not for God or others, but for myself. And I would have run away with Paul; I believe he loved me and we could have had a quiet home with a picket fence and jasmine by the front door.

If I had the chance to live again …

There was nowhere to be until 4:30, so she had time to walk on one of the trails surrounding campus, taking the long way home.

Saturday

5

Wherever you turn your eyes the world can shine like transfiguration. You don't have to bring a thing to it except a little willingness to see.

Marilynne Robinson, *Gilead*

Rex drove up about 5:30 — just like he'd said. Jordan had arrived a few minutes earlier and was waiting outside the church doors.

"You're a man of your word, Rex; rare bird. Great to see you this morning."

"It's a little early to start handing out halos. Five dozen cherry danishes; I'll help you carry them in."

"Sure, right this way." Jordan opened a side door and the two men toted the handmade treats into the kitchen; the boxes were still warm. "Rex, the people will really appreciate these, as do I. What do I owe you?"

Rex hemmed and hawed for a second. "How much cash you got in your pocket right now?"

Jordan was a little surprised, then embarrassed. "You're asking a minister how much cash he has?" He fumbled a moment and pulled out a five-dollar bill and two quarters. "Rex, I had intended to cut you a check."

"Tell you what — I'll take the five dollars. That plus the looks on the faces of those men yesterday morning when I delivered a danish to each one puts everything square. It was like they hadn't run into grace in a long, long time. They asked me, 'What are we supposed to do with these?' I said, 'Heck, eat 'em.' They were like a bunch of little boys after that, laughing and …"

Jordan thought he saw tears at the corners of Rex's eyes. He paused and asked, "You're sure about this?"

"As sure as grace. Listen, my wife and I talked as we prepared these; we might consider helping you like this, at least once a month. Give us time to think about it."

"Take the time you need. Really, thank you."

"Alright, enough chat. I've gotta go. I'll be in touch. Say, could I walk back through the sanctuary?"

It seemed an odd, but innocent request. "Sure. Through that hallway there and you're in; the front entrance is unlocked, just shut the …" Rex was gone with a wave before Jordan finished his sentence. Something about Rex's words and actions made Jordan curious; not suspicious, just curious.

Jordan tiptoed through the hall and stopped just short of the doorway to the sanctuary. He was surprised to see that Rex had lit one of the prayer candles stationed near the entrance; its gentle, warm glow provided just enough light to see Rex walking down the middle aisle, running his hand along the tops of pews, pausing a second, then continuing on. Sometimes a man walking down an aisle is simply that; this, however, seemed different. Rex moved with the rhythm of familiarity, like someone at home.

Jordan did what he could in the moment. He raised his hand in the arc of blessing and whispered into the sanctuary's shadows: "Mercy."

●●●

Jim and Linda stopped by the Dobbins' house on their way to the church. It was early, but they knew Sam and Phillip would be up, packing, trying to leave as soon as possible. Linda packed a bag full of deli sandwiches, chips, juice boxes, and some chocolate chip cookies — the slice-and-bake kind. They'd also picked up a few puzzle books for the twins and the new Pixar movie for all four of the girls.

"This will save you from fast food and maybe help you make a little better time. It feels small." Linda didn't quite know what else to say.

The four longtime friends embraced and held on just a little longer than usual. Jim insisted, "You'll call when you decide on the service, right?"

"You know we will, Jim," Phillip said. "Your first day at the Soup Kitchen?"

"We're supposed to meet Pastor Ross at seven. Jim, we'd better get going." Linda hugged Sam one last time and moved to her side of the car.

Jim shook Phillip's hand and left five twenty-dollar bills in it, folded just so. "Maybe that'll cover your gas getting there."

"Jim, you don't need …" But Jim shook Phillip's hand away.

"It's not what we should do, Phillip; it's what we *must* do. We're planning to come to the funeral. We'll see you then."

●●●

David woke up unusually early for a Saturday. He stood at Luci's bedside until she realized he was there. "David, it's still early."

"I can't go back to sleep. Will you read to me?"

Luci groaned a little. "Alright. Hop in."

Luci pulled back the comforter and made room for her youngest. He would usually tuck himself against her, mold himself as an extension of her. Luci loved moments like this. But he kept some distance this morning, enough to be noticeable. "Is something wrong, buddy?"

"Mom, Grandpa says a black man took his job; that's why he and Gran lost their house."

Initially drowsy, Luci was now wide awake. "That's what your grandpa says?"

"Yeah." David turned and backed up under Luci's arm, his usual snuggle position.

Luci could hear Kurt's voice: "Luce, if anything ever happens to me, raise our sons to be real." A single tear spilled down her cheek. The tear contained sadness, fear, anger, loneliness, resolve, and a prayer. She had no idea what it would look or sound like, but she determined to confront her father. It was time to start doing what she could to uphold her husband's legacy and break her father's. *Help me, Jesus.* Maybe it was time to start praying again too.

Luci looked down to see David had fallen asleep. She opened the book he brought to her bed and read:

> "It doesn't happen all at once," said the Skin Horse. "You become. It takes a long time.... But these things don't matter at all, because once you are Real you can't be ugly, except to people who don't understand."

●●●

Sam, Phillip, and the girls were on the road a few minutes before seven o'clock. The Trooper had only a half tank of gas, so Phillip decided to stop at the convenience store not far from their house. Given that it was early on a Saturday morning, the place was quiet save for a Greyhound-like bus loading and unloading passengers. As he pumped the gas, Phillip noticed two young girls step off the bus; they looked about Maggie's age. Their movements were jerky; their eyes gave away the emotion of the moment — fear, it was unmistakable. An older-model Audi pulled into the lot and a tall man got out on the passenger side; he directed the girls to the backseat. Then the car whisked them away. This all happened in the time it took for Phillip to unscrew the gas cap and choose the grade of gas to purchase; in other words, in no time at all.

●●●

Sam and Phillip had no way of knowing for certain, but their gut feeling was one of having witnessed a facet of sex trafficking. When a person is coerced, forced, or deceived into prostitution, or maintained in prostitution through coercion, that person is a victim of trafficking. Anyone involved in recruiting, transporting, harboring, receiving, or obtaining the person for that purpose has committed a trafficking crime. Sex trafficking can also occur alongside debt bondage, as women and girls are forced to continue in prostitution through the use of unlawful "debt" purportedly incurred through their transportation or recruitment — or their crude "sale" — which exploiters insist they must pay off before they can be free.

Sam and Phillip were startled because of the apparent ages of the girls. Estimates exist that as many as two million children are subjected to prostitution in the global commercial sex trade, even though the use of children in the commercial sex trade is prohibited under both U.S. law and the United Nations TIP Protocol. Sex trafficking has devastating consequences for minors, including long-lasting physical and psychological trauma, disease (including HIV/AIDS), drug addiction, unwanted pregnancy, malnutrition, social ostracism, and possible death. There are those who believe this problem to be something that happens in other parts of the world, not in America, in places like Santa Fe.

●●●

Phillip tapped on the window to get Sam's attention. He mouthed: "Did you see that?"

Sam cracked her door open. "Yes. Something about that didn't feel right."

Phillip didn't quite know how to say it. "That was like something on television. Those girls were no older than …"

"Maggie. I know. I'll go pay for the gas. Do you think we should report it?" Sam was a little shaken.

Sam went inside the store while Phillip called the police. He didn't know how to describe it other than to tell the officer what he'd seen, that it felt suspicious. The officer was grateful and took Phillip's cell number in case follow-up was needed.

Sam returned to the car. "What did the police say?"

"The officer took my story and my information, and thanked me for paying attention. But it didn't sound like much could be done. We didn't witness a crime being committed. For all we know, that could have been their aunt or something."

"You really believe that, Phillip?"

"Not for a minute. C'mon, let's get going."

As Sam and Phillip buckled up, Kate piped up from the back: "Dad, that man looks sad."

"What? What man, honey?" Phillip turned to see Kate pointing to the ice freezer by the store's entrance. There, as plain as day, sat a man in shirt sleeves, talking to no one at all. "He does look sad, Kate."

"Was he there when I walked in?" As Sam tried to remember, the man struggled to his feet and began to walk away. "How could I have missed him?"

Maggie had seen him as well. She raised her hand and waved, but he kept on walking.

●●●

"Wife and kids, Jesus H. Those were the days. No more." Louis watched the Trooper drive away. He was walking a little smoother, but his ribs still hurt. The nice hospital nurse had called him a cab, against Louis's wishes, and told the driver, "Take him where he wants to go, here in town." The only problem was Louis couldn't get back to where he wanted to go.

Louis was no riches-to-rags story; that would have been too easy. And life's not that easy. No, he was an insurance salesman with a wife and three kids who got caught up in heroin. He hadn't planned for it to happen. Louis believed nobody plans for trouble like that, but sometimes it happens. Some coworkers had dropped him home one night after a party; he was completely wasted. His wife confronted him and a fight began; his son, his only son, stepped in between them and Louis slapped him into the wall. He broke his son's jaw. That was a Wednesday. By Friday, the wife and kids were gone, good and gone.

Louis figured it was time to find a new place. He couldn't remember how long he'd been in Santa Fe. It didn't matter. "Those boys should'n'tve done that, Jesus H. Oh Jesus …"

Soup Kitchen. More than one church member had tried to persuade Jordan to refer to the ministry by some other name; maybe *House of Bread* or *Feed the Need* or something with pizzazz. But the young pastor consistently stood his ground. The model Jordan wanted Grace Church to follow was the soup kitchen of the 1930s: "No politics. No bull. Just soup." In the most recent discussions about the ministry's name, Jordan spoke plainly — "We're not trying to be great here, just good. Soup is good and we serve it out of a kitchen. What's so hard to understand?"

Grace Church stood in a long line of tradition. Soup kitchens have been providing nourishment to the poor and hungry since at least the eighteenth century. Though no longer serving solely a fare of soup and bread, they remain an important component of private food relief. The Great Depression of the 1930s ushered in a resurgence in soup kitchens. Along with breadlines, soup kitchens became a daily part of the life of millions. Their heyday waned, however, as government income, support, and food assistance programs were established.

Modern soup kitchen meals are typically free and unlike public food assistance programs usually do not have income or other eligibility requirements. The majority of soup kitchens are affiliated with larger nonprofits, most often that of churches, like Grace Church, which usually supply the facility and equipment, financial resources, food, and volunteers to staff the operation. Additional resources, most often in the form of food, are obtained from the local food bank, government commodity distribution programs, community retail outlets, and community food drives.

Soup kitchens serve a diverse group of people, including those who are homeless or unemployed, the working poor, public assistance recipients, the elderly, and people with health problems and disabilities. People often rely on these programs as a daily source of nourishment for many months, sometimes several years. For many people in Santa Fe, the Soup Kitchen provided such a source.

Over the years, soup kitchens have frequently been met with opposition. Contemporary critics claim that soup kitchens provide, at best, a short-term Band-Aid remedy to hunger;

however, they do not get at the root causes of hunger such as poverty, low wages, and lack of affordable housing. Many soup kitchen supporters readily concede that their approach may offer only a short-term response, but they argue it plays a vital role in trying to meet immediate food needs of the poor. Jordan would agree with this; in other words, if you're hungry, you're hungry.

●●●

Jim and Linda arrived with a group of others, ready to step into whatever this particular Saturday with these particular people held. Jordan gathered the new volunteers in the dining hall for a pep talk and handed them an 8½ x 11 sheet of paper with the recipe for the day: GRACE SOUP.

GRACE SOUP

Ingredients:

50 lbs. potatoes

35 lbs. ham — fresh not smoked ham — w/o bone, skin, or fat

35 lbs. onions

1200 oz. Campbell's cream of mushroom soup — try to use low-sodium as the regular is too salty

(there are 32 oz. in a commercial sized can, so you will need approx. 40 cans)

7½ lbs. barley

8 jars ham base (16 oz.) — use low-sodium and perhaps fewer jars or none

(carrots and celery are good to add and help to stretch the
soup)

Directions:

Preheat pots with enough water to cover the bottom.

Add barley with enough hot water to cover and cook
for 30 minutes.

Peel and slice potatoes about one inch thick.

Cut ham into cubes — no bones, fat, or skin.

Slice onions ¼- to ½-inch thick.

Add potatoes, ham, and onions with enough water to
cover. Add celery and carrots, if using.

Cook until potatoes start to soften.

Add soup and ham base to taste.

Once potatoes break down, lower heat.

"Today we're serving grace. Some of it will be in the form of
soup, some in the form of a smile, some in the form of learning someone's name, maybe even some in the form of leaving
someone alone. But it's all grace.

"This is your first time to serve and I couldn't be more thankful for your willingness to help us. I'd like to ask you to follow
the *to-to-for* rule today. First, pay attention *to* the people who
come, each and every one. Any time you can learn and then
call someone by name, fantastic. Second, pay attention *to* yourself; what you're feeling, thinking — are you getting frustrated
with something? Are you thoroughly enjoying something? And
third, pay attention *for* God. Trust me — he's already here.

"I've asked our veterans to pair up with each of you. They know what's going on; just follow their lead." As if on cue, the veterans emerged from the kitchen and sought out their shadows for the day. Some were members of Grace Church, some were people from the community, all were there of their own free will.

Jim and Linda waited for someone to approach them, but no one ever did. The rest of the newbies followed their leaders to begin setting up tables and mixing lemonade and dividing cherry danishes. Jordan walked over to where the Fairchilds were standing.

Linda was almost embarrassed. "Pastor Ross, we don't appear to have much of a leader."

Jordan smiled. "No, you don't have much of a leader, but you do have me. Why don't you and Jim stick close? I know almost everyone who regularly shows up. I can introduce you and you can learn some names. Names are very important."

"You've mentioned calling people by their names several times now," Jim stated.

"It's not always necessarily that you *call* names; it's more important, I believe, to learn their names. Tacking someone's name on the end of every question or statement is a little like breaking the third commandment." Jordan wondered if Jim or Linda knew which one was number three.

Jim reassured his faith. "Taking the Lord's name in vain?"

"Nice job, Jim. You can take the Lord's name in vain and you can also take a man or woman's name in vain. Some of the people who will show up here today have little else left besides their name. Treating that lightly or in some robotlike fashion is offensive; it doesn't have anything to do with grace."

"And that's what we're serving," Linda said.

Jordan chuckled. "Somebody's paying attention already. Listen, you two will do great today. I asked you to help us because I believe you love people. The people here today need love. It's a good match; not perfect, but good."

●●●

Even though he was their partner, Jordan could tell that Jim and Linda were still nervous. The serving began at eleven, but people started gathering about an hour before, getting their place in line. Jordan had been amazed lately at the ones in line; they did not fit the traditional picture of Soup Kitchen customers. He began introducing people to Jim and Linda. Some were reticent to talk, but many told their stories, maybe not the complete story, but enough that Jim and Linda felt it on their own skin. Among those they met were:

- *Leslie* — who had a freak accident and was hospitalized several days. The medicine and hospital stay left her with a $65,000 bill. Leslie has insurance, but like millions of Americans, she's underinsured; her company notified her they would pay only $3,000 of the bill. She's already behind on her payments.
- *Hector* — who has a part-time job as a courier but, after his rent and utilities, has little left for food. He may be

moving on soon as a friend told him of some good jobs in Oregon. He'd like to get married someday or start a blog.

- *Freda* — who along with her three sons were displaced by Hurricane Katrina. She works two jobs — as a marketer and a cashier. "The people of Santa Fe really opened their arms, but the elected officials didn't do squat." She misses New Orleans.

- *Tammy and Jeff* — a married couple who both work at Wal-Mart, she part-time and he full-time. Their seven-year old son, Tyler, has had multiple surgeries after a dog bite. Tyler is doing better, but Tammy and Jeff seem to be arguing a lot these days.

Linda excused herself for a moment from the flow of people gathering. As she stood and looked in the bathroom mirror, she found it almost hard to breathe. And then the tears came. How could she have missed all these people, right here in her town? America was supposed to be the land of opportunity, a place where anyone could apply themselves and do better. On this day, in the Soup Kitchen, that kind of thinking felt like the rhetoric of the privileged.

Jordan watched and waited for Linda to return. "Are you going to be okay?" He was concerned; sometimes these initial experiences could almost overwhelm.

"No, Pastor Ross, I'm not okay. And it feels right to not be." Linda walked back to where Jim was talking with another guest at the Kitchen.

Jordan had no desire to overdramatize the moment, but he felt a slight shift in the balance of the things of this earth. Linda would not be okay and because of that, others, maybe orphans, maybe the poor in that very room, maybe even those yet unborn, might be noticed for who they were — the *hijos de Dios* — the children of God.

●●●

Jordan kept an eye open for a David Letterman jacket, but Louis never showed up. Jordan wondered, *How do we live with what we know?* And then, *How do we live with what we don't know?* These were deep, soul-rending questions, the likes of which ministers and poets and maybe artists wrestle. There would always be time for such askings; now was time to bless and break the danishes.

Jordan prayed over five dozen cherry danishes, the first time in his pastoral career. He asked the God who said *Blessed are the poor* to bless both the hands that prepared and the hands that received. The volunteers distributed the pastries, but this time there were no baskets left over — yet the miracle was that there was just enough.

●●●

The woman had always said, "You're mine." At first, she saw it as ownership; she provided for the little lost girl, so the girl owed her. But somewhere along the way, the words took on new meaning. It wasn't a sudden change, but more like something that crept slowly along, unnoticed, until it had grown strong and undeniable. The woman never spoke the new feelings; she kept them hidden. If the feelings dropped from her lips, the girl-no-more named Isabel might feel a freedom to go away, maybe for good. The woman feared such thoughts. If Isabel left, she would be all alone.

When Isabel had not returned home last night, the woman stood outside the house, looking, searching, hoping. She was not one who prayed, but uncontrollable words surfaced in her head: *Please, please … I'll do anything.*

The woman remembered those first mornings so long ago now, mothering the little girl alone and afraid. Isabel used to tell her that all she really wanted was a quiet home surrounded by a white picket fence with jasmine blooming by the door. She wondered how the little girl had imagined such a thing. She remembered one particular morning, a Christmas Day when they took a walk in the brown hills surrounding town. She had told Isabel, "We'll walk an absolutely straight line and see what we find." They walked their straight line and came upon a fifty-dollar bill out in the middle of nowhere. How it got there is anyone's guess. It did not matter. Isabel's excitement at the treasure made it the best day of the woman's life.

The woman wondered if she might find Isabel if she walked another absolutely straight line.

6

May God bless my people … oh, remember them kindly in their time of trouble; and in their hour of taking away.

James Agee,
A Death in the Family

The people left at about the same pace they arrived; by two almost everyone was gone. There had been no problems to speak of; a couple of men argued once and a woman screamed at the volunteer dispensing soup, but those things were mild, expected. Jordan's apprentices for the day had done well. Jim and Linda seemed to be fully present with the people — heart, mind, soul, and strength. There would be time for further reflection later, but he did want to thank them before teardown and cleanup absorbed everyone.

"Jim, Linda, thank you both for being here today. Well done."

Jim shook his pastor's hands with both hands, the way a man would shake hands with someone he was grateful to and for. "We'll be here next time, Pastor."

Linda nodded in agreement. "What *is,* is enough, isn't it? It just needs a hand."

Jim and Linda didn't recognize the ponytailed man approaching them. But Jordan did. "Rex, your pastries were a hit. Jim, Linda, this is the man behind the cherry danishes."

Jordan's cell phone rang and he stepped aside as Rex and the Fairchilds greeted one another. Only Jordan's ears could hear these words:

"Pastor, this is Sergeant Hankins with the police department. We've met once or twice. I hate to bother you on a Saturday, but something's happened and I feel we need your help, probably in more ways than one. I've got a car on the way to pick you up, alright?"

Jordan was used to providing pastoral care to the community when needed; he told the officer to have the car come around to the front of the church, he would be waiting. He informed the three new friends as to what was going on and started to excuse himself, but then turned and faced Rex. "Why did you stop by?"

"I'm not quite sure, Pastor. I thought … maybe I could help with the cleanup."

Jordan was having almost the same feelings he'd had when Rex dropped off the pastries early that morning; however, now the curiosity was suspicion. "Rex, I might be able to use your help, if you're offering. We might be awhile."

"I'll tell the others. You go ahead," Jim said. "We'll make sure everything is clean and locked up."

●●●

An older patrolman picked up the two men within minutes. Jordan started to introduce his companion, but the officer got there first. "Rex, long time no see."

"It has been, hasn't it, Will? Your family is well?"

"Lord, yes. The girls are almost grown now. Time flies whether you're having fun or not."

"Yes, it does." Rex introduced his companion. "Will Jennings, meet the pastor of Grace Church — Jordan Ross."

"Nice to meet you, Pastor. It's good that ..." The police radio roared to life and the officer returned to his focus, informing dispatch, "We're just blocks away."

Jordan turned to the man beside him in the backseat: "I don't even know your last name."

"Chatham, Rex Chatham."

The patrol car parked near the campus, where a crowd appeared to be gathering. Officer Jennings escorted the two men beyond waist-high ribbons of yellow tape and reporters. Sergeant Hankins stepped out from among a cluster of policemen and greeted Jordan with a handshake and a questioning look at Rex.

"This is Rex Chatham, Sergeant. I asked him to come," Jordan said.

Officer Jennings added: "He can help, Sergeant."

Sergeant Hankins took one step closer to the men, tightening the gap between them. "Please follow me. I'll talk as we walk. Some students were out jogging this morning and found a body. It's a female, hard to tell her age exactly; but what's not hard to tell is that someone, maybe more than one, beat her." The men were getting closer to a cluster of scrub oak. "She was stripped of any clothing, except for a jacket draped over her; there's quite a bit of blood; it looks like the assailant dragged her to this spot." The sergeant turned and looked at Jordan. "Pastor, the jacket has your name inside." Then he pointed to the edge of a washout.

Jordan looked down to see his weather-beaten Letterman jacket covering the torso and partially hidden face of a woman. It could not hide the blood. Jordan was suddenly afraid — *Louis*.

The woman's legs were crumpled beneath her, yet the legs looked like those of a child. Rex Chatham managed to ask, "May I see her face?" As the jacket was lowered to reveal the eyes of the dead, Rex knew; there are some things you do not forget — *Isabel*.

The sergeant spoke into the silence. "Pastor Ross, was your jacket stolen or anything in the past?"

Jordan gathered his courage: "I gave it to one of the men who visits our Soup Kitchen. Louis; I have no last name. I cannot believe he ..."

"How long ago was this, Pastor?" Sergeant Hankins was taking notes.

"Long enough," Jordan replied. "I can give you a physical description."

As Jordan spoke to the sergeant, Officer Jennings moved toward the man he knew; it was obvious Rex was shaken. "Rex, did you know this woman?"

"My God. Yes, Will ... but only for a couple of days, years ago. She told us her name was Isabel."

"You're sure, Rex?"

"Yes ... I'm sure."

The sergeant spoke again. "Pastor Ross, I also asked you to come for the young ladies. A couple of college girls found the body; they're pretty shaken up. Could you speak with them? One of them asked for you specifically."

●●●

Jordan walked a short distance to find Elly and her room-mate, Kris, being interviewed by an officer. He approached and made eye contact with Elly, who managed a tentative smile. The officer had what he needed, for now; he asked, "Pastor Ross?" Jordan nodded. "Good. Girls, just stay close for awhile."

Jordan extended his hands to Elly and Kris; they took them and for the next few moments the two young women cried. There was no verbal pastoral care to give, no words to say; just the ministry of presence, being there, and letting the tears fall where they may.

After the wave of grief had settled a little, Elly looked back toward the body: "Pastor Ross, who would do such a horrible thing? She was so … beautiful."

People usually asked Jordan *why* bad things happened; in this case, Elly was asking him *who*. The truth was, he did know. Jordan Ross knew that many people these days were really agnostic about God; oh, they might believe in him, but few trusted. And while many believed prayers were answered, they refused to listen to the answers. There has been too much hurt, too much suffering. We the people are not of the peace-able kingdom, not yet at least; in fact, some days there is little if any peace here. But there is a great deal of anger and violence and lust and greed, hands reaching for throats at all hours of the day and night; some of them reaching for baseball bats to silence those who are beautiful.

It's like the rain and the mesquite tree. The heat builds and the leaves droop, but clouds are off in the distance. They come on slowly, but they do come with the promise of rain. This gradual promise goes on for days, weeks, sometimes longer. But there are times when the rain does not fall, when the monsoon skips. Yet the mesquite still stands and believes, waits; the spring rains will come one day. But the mesquite is a tree; people are not trees. If the promise is delayed or skips us for some reason, we stop believing, we refuse to wait, we take matters into our own hands, not realizing we do not hold time or seasons in our grasp. But we do hold the power of life and death. Who *would* do such a thing? For some, the rains have not fallen for months, years, lifetimes; their eyes are completely dry. Who *could* do such a thing? It could be anyone.

"Elly ..." But then Jordan stopped. He would not speak his many thoughts, not now; only this one — "Yes, Elly, she was beautiful."

●●●

Sergeant Hankins thanked Jordan for his help, both the information and talking with the girls. Jordan turned to go and remembered Rex; he was still standing at the scene. "Rex, the sergeant says we can go."

Rex spoke over his shoulder. "How much money you got in your pocket?"

Jordan had already heard that question once today — was Rex joking? "What … well, I've got two quarters. It's what you left me."

"Good," Rex said. "I'll take them." He reached out a hand and Jordan deposited the coins. "Sergeant, may I close the eyes of the dead?"

"Why, Mr. Chatham?" The sergeant then answered his own question: "My grandmother used to say that if the eyes of the dead remain open, we might see our own death captured in their eyes."

"I guess that might be true," Rex said. "But it just seems like a fitting way to say 'good-night.'"

The sergeant could tell the man was serious; so could Jordan. "Yes, it seems right."

Jordan watched as Rex closed the woman's eyelids and gently placed a quarter on each. Then he heard his new friend speak old words: "May God bless Isabel in the hour of her taking away."

<hr />

What Sergeant Hankins and Pastor Ross and Rex and Elly and Kris would never know is what was now locked in the shared minds of a homeless man named Louis who had just boarded a bus to somewhere other than Santa Fe and a young lady in the last moments of her life.

Earlier that morning a truck had made a U-turn in front of the convenience store and pulled up beside him. A man and two young girls approached him and asked if they might help him on his way. The man handed Louis five twenty-dollar bills, folded just so. It was enough for a bus ride to some place where he might forgive himself and forget her face.

It was late Friday afternoon when the boys jumped out of the scrub oak. She guessed they had been watching her, waiting for her. There were two of them, maybe sixteen years old. The look in the boys' eyes reminded Isabel of years ago, days when the suffering seemed so great. She started to scream but suddenly could not find the breath; another boy, even older, had stepped from behind and hit her across the back with a baseball bat. The next moments were primarily the smell of boys and alcohol. Then they were gone; she thought they were finished. Isabel struggled to her knees. She had endured worse. But then the oldest came back. His eyes were dry, parched; they had not seen rain in a long time.

"So you think you're better than me, huh? You stupid ..."

She felt the bat come down hard on her shoulder and then at the base of her neck. The previous moments had been smell, but these were about sight. At first, Isabel saw nothing but black, dark shadows. It was terrifying. But then they came, the bright orange and white shapes darting back and forth ... her angels.

She had always wondered how much more suffering there was to be beautiful. Finally Isabel's dream came to pass, but the beauty was too much for one to bear.

Louis stepped into the clearing. The boy had stripped Isabel's body of clothing and was trying to drag her to the edge of a washout. Louis yelled, "Jesus H.!" The boy looked at him and just laughed. He held her clothes and said, "You're both too late." Two other boys emerged from the trees and then they were gone.

"Jesus H. Christ! Those boys shouldn't've done this! Oh Jesus! Jesus!" Louis looked around for someone, anyone, but he was all alone — the homeless man and a woman-girl half-dead. He had no idea what to do. "Jesus H., help ..." He knelt close to her; he had no idea who she was. Then he closed his eyes and did what he could:

"You lie down ... beside still waters ... mercy shall follow. Amen."

Louis struggled with the jacket the preacher had given him, but he finally wiggled free and placed it over her. He had to leave; someone would be coming soon. "I'm sorry." He began to walk away but turned for one last look at her face; there was something about her, something lovely.

Epilogue

Sunday's child is full of grace …

Sunday had been a comin'. Now it was here. Jordan had planned on it being a full but manageable weekend; however, the plans of mice and men and ministers often go awry. He'd asked Rex the night before what happened to the weekend. His new friend answered without pause: "Life." Rex then proceeded to tell Jordan what he thought the young pastor needed to know, what he was due. About how after Isabel had gone, he had walked away from the old church after the following Sunday's service, never to return. How he and his wife had heard the rumors: that his breakdown was due to health concerns or, worse, an indiscretion brought on by improper boundaries. And, then, what had really prompted his departure.

As Jordan raised his cup to take the last draw of coffee, he looked at his sermon notes on the table: an introductory story, quotes from old dead men, and a threadbare story about a Samaritan. It all seemed so shallow in light of Isabel's death. He spit the coffee back in the cup — lukewarm. Jordan was afraid the people might do the same with his sermon.

He answered the door, not sure who would be knocking quite this early. Jordan opened the door to find his new friend holding a coffee and a danish. "Good morning, Rex."

"Hi. I thought after last night you might be doubting yourself this morning."

Jordan accepted the gifts. "Thanks. How'd you guess? Can you stay a minute?"

"No, I've got somewhere to go. Listen, just remember you're not responsible for what you don't know, but what you do know. The people need to hear from you today."

"You're sure?" Jordan asked.

"I'm sure of grace, Pastor. Beyond that, it gets fuzzy."

◦◦◦

Luci got up early to make chocolate chip pancakes for the boys, their favorite. It's what Kurt would do if he were here. She'd had no idea what you do on the first anniversary of your husband's death, that is until Elly called. Luci thought her new friend's suggestion of a picnic on campus was a wonderful idea. They were to meet Elly about 11:30, so she and the boys could have a leisurely breakfast together.

Everything was going fine until Luci opened the closet door to get a robe. For some reason, the clothes had been hung in a way that left Kurt's old flannel shirt exposed. Luci removed the shirt from the hanger and smelled it, even though it had been washed several times since he'd worn it last. Still, she was convinced it smelled like him. Luci took the shirt off the hanger

Epilogue

and wrapped it around her; then she sat down on the floor and cried.

●●●

Sam stepped outside the funeral home for some fresh air. Seeing her dad lying there like that made it all real. Not that it hadn't been before, but seeing his body made it different.

Ben saw his sister leave and followed her outside. "Have you thought about what I mentioned — a legacy for Dad, something that matters?"

"Yes, Ben, I have. There are two or three groups I'd like to suggest to you that are doing work that seems to be helping people. One is a small organization that Phillip will be working with. He says the young man leading the group needs some help. I'll tell you about the other two later. But listen, if there's any left over ... well, you may think this is silly, but I'd like to give it to the church here and designate it for ... for a koi pond."

"A koi pond? For Central Baptist Church? Here in Kansas?"

"I just want you to think about it. Dad liked watching the koi at St. John's; I remember he said they were 'lovely as angels.' Maybe somebody around here needs a place like that to sit and pray or dream or something. Maybe."

Ben put his arm around his older sister, his only sister, and chuckled. "Alright. Let's look into it. You do realize some of these boys around here will try to fish that pond." Ben turned away, paused for a second, and then started to speak again. "Sam, I was secretly a little upset when you and Phillip didn't come right away. I told you to stay, but I still wanted you here. I wasn't lying, but I wasn't completely honest. But I obviously didn't understand everything that was going on. This morning Kate told me all about Luci. I'm glad you stayed, Sam. Dad really would be proud of that."

"Kate told you? Figures. Ben, don't worry. Trust me when I say it was hard not to drop everything and come, it really was. I guess I was able to stay because I've been living a pretty middle-of-the-road life for awhile now, and though I used to think of that as a quiet place, a place of safety and comfort, I've come to realize that it's about to kill me. I've found myself getting upset at things I shouldn't, sometimes just plain angry; trying to live a balanced, middle-of-the-road kind of life will do that to you, or at least it was doing it to me. Life is … over in the edges, off to the sides, messy, but good messy. It wasn't that somebody was trying to ruin my plans, but that somebody, namely God, was trying to get my attention. Anyway, my daughters deserve more than a mother with low-grade cynicism. But I had to stop some things in order to get started. That may not make sense, but it's what I've had to do. Staying for Luci was one of those things."

"It does, Sam. It probably makes more sense than you know." The brother and his sister sat down on the curb while the Kansas wind blew, as always. "Dad liked the koi pond, huh?"

"He did. You do know you've never been out to visit. Come see us. I'd like that. We're the tallest trees in our forest now, Ben."

"I thought about that."

●●●

Rex walked back to the car to get an umbrella for his wife. The sun was out strong; it was going to be warm in Santa Fe. Before he made his way back, he silently uttered a prayer for his young pastor friend: *He's a good man, Lord … full of mercy. Give him courage this morning. Please.*

He saw her turn and motion for him to c'mon. *Amen.* Rex meandered through the cemetery, sidestepping the stones that marked the dead. Today they brought fresh jasmine to Isabel's marker. Before it had always been roses, but Rex smelled the blooms the day before at the Soup Kitchen and thought it time for a change. His wife agreed.

He opened the umbrella and held it to shade his wife while she placed the flowers on the grave just so. "Yes, Rex, these are beautiful." They stood there for a few moments, the sun getting warmer. "Rex, do you really believe God doesn't put more on a person than they can bear?"

"It sure feels like he does sometimes. I'm not sure I know beans about God. But maybe he wants us to stop and help each other. If we don't, what he puts on us just might be too much."

"That's what I think too." His wife put her hand in his and they walked back to the car under the umbrella. As Rex opened her door, she said, "You could help him, you know; be close by in case he falls."

Rex drew a breath. "Like you were for me?"

She smiled and he shut her door. He walked around the front of the car so she could see him; she always liked for him to do that.

●●●

Jordan stepped to the pulpit with indecision still dogging his thoughts. But then maybe Rex was right. He voiced a silent prayer for mercy and stepped into it:

"My friends, I don't have a sermon for you this morning. I know that will disappoint some and thrill others, so 'I'm sorry' and 'you're welcome.' I tried to prepare a sermon on the familiar. Instead, I've decided to tell you a story on the not-so-familiar.

"One day a man, a good man, a godly man, was taking out the trash when he saw a young woman lying by the side of a dumpster. She'd had a life growing within her, but the life died, and so, in a way, she was dying too; she was half-dead. Although she looked like a child herself, she was not. Her eyes told the story of years of suffering. This good man dropped all of his plans, everything that everyone around him thought so important, and took her in his arms and carried her home. The man and his wife nursed the young woman, doing what they could, praying as best they knew how. The woman regained enough strength to tell the man and his wife her name: *Isabel*.

"What the woman did not know was that many years before, the good man and his wife had a little girl named Isabel. They had dreamed of her; only God knew how much they loved her. One Sunday morning, as the good man prepared to go and speak of holy things, he backed out of the garage and did not see Isabel playing behind the car. She was rushed to the hospital, but her injuries were too severe. Isabel died.

"The good man dreamed that one day God would give Isabel back to them. And so, when Isabel was found among the trash, this man believed his dream-prayers had finally been answered. But after two days of caring for her, the man and his wife awoke to find Isabel was gone. It was sadness upon sadness, simply too great. The man found he could no longer speak of holy things; he counted himself among the half-dead.

"One day, the half-dead man met another man who spoke of holy things, and he said to himself, 'If you cannot speak of holy things, maybe you can do holy things.' And so the half-dead man did try, and one thing led to another and maybe the God who is great and the God who is good saw those holy things and believed they were as good as words, maybe better.

"The man who spoke of holy things asked for his help; a woman had been killed, and in the face of grief, two together are stronger than one. As the two men stood before the young woman's body, the good man, the man God still believed in, realized it was Isabel. Whether or not it was his daughter was not the point; her name was Isabel.

"If you were to ask this man, this good man, about this story today he would say, 'There are our plans, which most of us confidently travel in the direction of, and then there is life, usually somewhere off to the side, asking us to pause and really live. I longed to hold my daughter throughout her life, but that was not to be the story. I did hold her at the beginning and in some way I was able to hold her again in the middle, when she had been discarded, almost lost … and I was able to hold her again at the end, to tell her good-bye and how beautiful she was.'"

And it was then that Jordan Ross, pastor of Grace Church, began to weep. He wept for good friends in Kansas who were at that very moment standing before a casket holding a beloved father. He wept for a young college girl, gifted with the compassion of the saints of old, who now lived in fear of a violent world that had suddenly become much closer. He wept for a military widow and her two sons who were this very day observing the anniversary of the death of their most loved soldier. He wept for a man without a home who was just moving into a new town with new faces but possibly the same old prejudices. He wept for a woman named Isabel and the suffering she endured at the hands of those who used her and those who ignored her — a woman who in this very second he prayed was safely in the arms of Jesus. And the pastor wept for a good man, a godly man, who was not far away placing fresh jasmine on the grave of a little girl that he and his wife hoped to see again one day, some day, when everything that is broken is pieced back together again and everything is beautiful.

Jordan did his best to compose himself. He remembered Rex's words: *The people need to hear from you.* As he wiped his eyes, he looked out at the people of Grace Church. Not all, but many were standing, each with an outstretched arm, as if holding up their pastor because suffering is often too great for one man or one woman to bear alone. It always has been.

Jordan concluded with some lines Phillip had shared with him: "For it is important that awake people be awake ... the darkness around us is deep. Amen."

●●●

The old white pickup with a new fuel pump on it pulled up along the sidewalk that circled the campus. Luci and her boys got out, all on the driver's side. Elly had said to meet her just outside the student center. As they headed up the sidewalk, Kurt Jr. said, "So Daddy was killed a year ago?"

Luci stopped. "Yes. Today is the anniversary of his death. Let's keep walking, okay?"

"That's Daddy's shirt, isn't it? Don't you miss him?" David asked.

"Yes, it's your daddy's shirt. I like it."

"Me too," David said.

"David, I miss him so much it hurts. But we're going to make it."

As they rounded the corner by the student center, they saw Elly sitting on a grassy hill. Luci thought she looked smaller for some reason; maybe she was tired. Elly waved hello and then motioned for the boys to c'mon. "Go ahead. Tell her I'll be right there."

Kurt Jr. and David only ran a short distance when Luci saw them stop and point. As she got closer to them, Luci noticed Elly was walking toward them from the other side. They both stopped where the boys were standing, beside a small garden pond filled with bright orange and white koi. "Look how big they are!" shouted David. "Can we have our picnic right here?"

"Sure," Elly said. "Kurt, would you please go get my basket?" Luci's oldest was gone before he could answer. "David, you might help him. It's heavy."

Luci's youngest ran after his brother as the koi gathered at the pond's edge, hoping to be fed.

Next Steps

Could you have saved Isabel? Or helped Louis regain his dignity and find a more comfortable and loving way to live out his life? Perhaps your role would have been that of Luci's best friend, providing comfort and support after Kurt's death and then sticking by her side and helping her build a new life of hope and faith.

Maybe you want to be that person, but you don't know how or where to start. We'd like to help. Why? Because God wants all of us to show love toward each other. One way we can show you that love is by helping you learn how to become a Good Samaritan.

Here are some suggestions:

1. Open a Bible and read Jesus' parable of the Good Samaritan in Luke 10:25 – 37. Put yourself in the shoes of all of the characters. Meditate on the story and pray through it until it pierces your heart.
2. Talk to those people with whom you "do life" about how they are involved in helping others. Sometimes we assume that the people we know live life similarly. If you ask around, you may discover that this is rarely the case!
3. Ask yourself, "What breaks my heart?" Hidden in this question may be the exact place God is calling you to start serving others.

4. Do research. There are many great national and international organizations doing things throughout the world to help others. Use your local library and the Internet to find resources to educate yourself, and then pick one issue that you're passionate about … and get involved!

5. Look around and begin to see all the opportunities that God is placing in your path. Then think about how you can press the "pause button" on your life so that you will be ready to respond to the needs God has placed before you.

6. Volunteer — perhaps at a local homeless shelter, food pantry, or soup kitchen. Most of these organizations are chronically understaffed and they will be excited to have you volunteer your time.

Another great way you can start is by visiting *www.startproject .org* and learning about start> Project, a growing movement of Good Samaritans who believe that loving others and changing the world starts today. One thing you will discover on the website is the *start> Becoming a Good Samaritan* six-session small group and church curriculum. Hosted by John Ortberg and featuring Christian leaders from around the world, it tackles these important topics:

- Becoming a Good Samaritan
- Caring for the Sick
- Seeking Justice and Reconciliation
- Honoring the Poor

- Tending to God's Creation
- Loving the Forsaken

In addition, the website features the necessary resources for small group use and the tools to launch a church-wide campaign.

●●●

How will you respond to this book? We have no idea! But we're sure God is already working in your heart, seeking to ignite a desire to be his visible hands, feet, and hope to a world thirsting for a cup of water, a loaf of bread, or freedom from slavery and oppression. You can be a person who makes a difference! You probably won't change the whole world … but you can say, "God, I saw what you prepared for me; I listened to your call; and I did my small but important part today. Help me to see … and do … again tomorrow."

The world God created has been tragically marred by the disharmony of sin and strife. But what was accomplished through the life, death, and resurrection of Jesus Christ is the restoration of that harmony. What has begun will be fulfilled upon his return. But in the space between, our lives must echo the words of Jesus: "Your kingdom come, your will be done … on earth as it is in heaven."

> Yesterday is gone.
> Tomorrow is not yet come.
> We have only today.
> Let us begin.
>
> Mother Teresa

Sources

NOTE: The factual information included in this story was provided by the following sources:

www.americanwidowproject.org

www.avert.org

www.cleanwateriniative.org

www.creationcare.org

www.emoregon.org/theologica_dialogue.php (Archbishop Tutu's story)

www.gladwell.com (*The Tipping Point: How Little Things Can Make a Big Difference*, Back Bay Books, 2002)

www.huffingtonpost.com

www.ijm.org

www.kibogroup.org

www.militarywidows.org

www.nationalhomeless.org

www.nlchp.org/

www.npr.org

www.pbs.org/now/

www.rodneystark.com/ (*The Rise of Christianity: How the Obscure, Marginal, Jesus Movement Became the Dominant Religious Force*, HarperOne, 1997)

www.thenation.com

www.unicef.org

www.usmayors.org

www.u-s-history.com

www.womensfundingnetwork.org

●●●

The "more" quote spoken by Jordan Ross on pages 30–31 comes from Madeleine L'Engle's *Walking on Water: Reflections on Faith and Art* (Shaw Books, 1980, p. 134).

And the reference to strawberry rhubarb pie comes from the heart and wisdom of Garrison Keillor.

> ## What does it take to "love your neighbor" in a global community?

start> Becoming a Good Samaritan

Six Sessions

Hosted by John Ortberg

Partnering with World Vision and the C2 Group, Zondervan presents a new DVD study, *start> Becoming a Good Samaritan* — an unprecedented initiative to help Christians live out Christ's love in world-changing ways right where they live.

This groundbreaking training program helps small groups, families, entire churches, and organizations of every size explore the most pressing issues of our time — then start actually doing something about them. Join teacher, speaker, and award-winning author John Ortberg as he hosts six emotionally packed sessions featuring a remarkable array of global Christian leaders, including Eugene Peterson, Philip Yancey, Matthew Sleeth, Jim Cymbala, Chuck Colson, Archbishop Desmond Tutu, Brenda Salter McNeil, Kay Warren, Joni Eareckson Tada, Rob Bell, Shane Claiborne, and many others.

Designed for use with the *start> Becoming a Good Samaritan Participant's Guide*, the *start> Becoming a Good Samaritan DVD* takes Christians out of the pews and into the streets where, as the hands and feet of Christ, they will live out the gospel, positively affecting those suffering from poverty, social injustice, pandemic diseases, and more. Visit www.just-start.org to learn about the nationwide church campaign experience. You'll also learn about the growing list of national and international supporters and have access to supplemental resources for the DVD curriculum.

Available in stores and online!